MW01133396

ASSISTED SUICIDE
OR
MURDER?
PRESTON BOURNE SAGA BEGINS

LAURN SMITH

authorHOUSE®

AuthorHouse™
1663 Liberty Drive
Bloomington, IN 47403
www.authorhouse.com
Phone: 833-262-8899

Published by AuthorHouse 11/08/2022

ISBN: 978-1-6655-7472-3 (sc)
ISBN: 978-1-6655-7470-9 (hc)
ISBN: 978-1-6655-7471-6 (e)

Library of Congress Control Number: 2022920269

Print information available on the last page.

CHAPTER 1

MY SANDTON EXPERIENCE BEGINS

I am Preston Bourne, and ex-chemical engineer. With no family and few friends, I moved to Sandton to hide from myself and the world. Sandton is an ordinary, medium-sized southern town in South Carolina with the usual Home Depot, Lowes, Costco, and Sam's Club and a shopping mall. Church steeples line the old main street, and a few are scattered in the suburbs. Upper-class homes surround the country club's golf course and lake. Sandton has the typical crime rate, a not-so-well-to-do side of town, and homeless people, but seems like a great place to live, raise a family and retire. I was simply looking to escape from my old world and find a new life.

I found a clean, modest hotel with a restaurant and bar and moved in. What happened next was not planned, was not pretty, and was totally out of character for me. I isolated myself in the hotel and started drinking too much, partially because I had nothing else to do. Honestly, drinking helped dull my memories of my past.

After a couple of weeks, I discovered that my house equity

money was evaporating faster than I had planned. I knew I had to find some type of work that was not engineering—my previous profession. I left the hotel to explore the town.

One night while in a bar near my hotel, I found a table and got my first Yuengling. I had only taken a few sips when a stocky, middle-aged policeman walk into the bar, glanced at me curiously, got a beer and wandered over to my table.

The policeman said, "You must be new around here. I know just about everybody. Do you mind if I join you"?

I replied, "Not at all, have a seat". *Why not? I had nothing to hide and no one else to talk to.*

"I'm Sergeant Jim Carson of the Sandton police department." He extended his hand, and we shook.

"Preston Bourne, pleased to meet you, sergeant.

"What brings you to our fair city, Preston?"

I responded, "Getting out of Oklahoma."

The sergeant laughed. "What kind of work do you do?" By this time, both of our beers were about empty, so he ordered two more beers.

"I'm concentrating on handyman work, but I'm not sure what I will settle on."

"Your hands are soft for an odd-job man" said the sergeant.

"You must be a detective! I'm still in the planning stages. I admitted I had been an engineer but had tired of it and wanted a change. Hence, the move to Sandton and my change of vocation".

We continued with small talk and got the third round of beers. He told me he had been on the police force for 35 years and grew up in Sandton. We sipped our beers for a couple of quiet moments.

He then asked, "How could you give up working as an engineer to work as a jack-of-all-trades since the salary difference would undoubtedly be significant?"

I said, "It's a long story. It may require a fourth beer. We order another round. The beer was beginning to have an effect on me, so after the beer arrived, I started telling him what happened in Texas. I told him I had been an engineer and owned a small engineering company. I told him about the death of the operator in the plant my company had designed and that I somehow felt I was responsible. I told him I had no family and just decided to relocate to Sandton. He was very sympathetic and said I could not blame myself for someone else's mistake. He asked me what I had done before owning the engineering company. For some unexplained reason, probably the beer, I also told him about my time as a marine sniper.

He was interested in life as a sniper and started asking questions. I told him I was not allowed to say much about it, and he seemed to accept that. As we got ready to leave the bar, he said he might know of some future handyman work that could surface in the next 2 or 3 weeks. I gave him my phone number. He asked where I was staying, so I told him I was staying at the Holiday Inn Express, close to the bar.

CHAPTER 2

MORE JOB OPPORTUNITIES

The next afternoon, I decided to do more looking around Sandton. It was a well-kept town, with clean streets, and reasonably new buildings. In addition, the streets appear to have been well laid out to handle the traffic – a good thing because I need to drive around looking for odd jobs.

As I was driving around, I passed Smitty's Bar and Grill. I decided to have a few beers and a local hamburger, so I turned around and went back to Smitty's. It was a small bar but had a great, cozy atmosphere. I sat at the bar so I could talk to the bartender about the town. I introduced myself to the bartender. He said," Welcome Preston Bourne. I am Danny Smith, owner of this bar and grill. I have never seen you here. Are you here on business or just passing through?"

I told him I had just moved to Sandton a few weeks ago. I ordered a hamburger and a Dos XX Lager beer.

Danny told me about Sandton. He said the population was approximately 40,000 and was mainly an agricultural and business center. He said there were not many heavy industrial plants in the immediate area.

My food order arrived, and I took a bite of the hamburger. I mentioned that it was the best hamburger I had eaten lately. Danny said his cook prided himself on blending and seasoning the meat. He has been with me for 15 years. He asked what type of work I did.

I took another bite of the hamburger to give myself time to consider my answer. I did not want to repeat my mistake of talking too much as I had with Sgt. Carson. I finally said I had been an engineer, but I got tired of that and decided to start over here. I told him I thought I would look for work as a handyman.

He studied me for what seemed like an eternity but was likely only 30 seconds. He finally said he knew someone that had bought an old house and that she might have some handyman work. He gave me her name, Samantha Carter, and her phone number. He said to call her and tell her that Danny Smith said to call her. He also said that she may not need help immediately and that she was very "picky" about her work.

I finished my meal and had a second beer. I told Danny that I appreciated his recommendation to call Ms. Carter and that I would. I then left the bar and headed back to my hotel. I decided that Sandton was beginning to seem like a friendly place to escape from my past.

I called Samantha Carter the next day and told her of my conversation with Danny Smith. She remarked that they were old friends and that she indeed did have some handyman work. She said she would be glad to meet with me. I told her that I had just moved to Sandton. I was available to meet with her anytime at her convenience. She suggested that I come by at 3:00 that afternoon, if possible. I got her address and told her I would see her at 3:00.

I arrived just before 3:00. It was an old, but grand home. It had a wrap-around porch, wood plank siding, a well-landscaped yard, and a large three-car garage. It looked like there was an apartment above the garage. The large oak trees around the house indicated that the house had been there for many years and that the people that built it were likely wealthy.

She was sitting on the front porch when I pulled into the driveway. I was expecting a middle-aged or older, wealthy lady based on the neighborhood, but she was anything but middle-aged. She looked to be in her middle-to-late thirties. She was dressed in blue jeans and a white pullover. She looked like a model from a fashion magazine. I have to admit that she was quite stunning.

I could only hope that I did not stutter when I spoke. I introduced myself and mentioned how I had met Danny. I told her I had just moved to Sandton and was planning to do handyman work. She asked what brought me to Sandton, so I told her I was tired of Oklahoma City and randomly chose a small southern town. I added that it seemed to be just the change I needed.

Our conversation changed to the work she needed. I interjected, "Will your husband be joining us?" She grinned and said she was not married. I felt like I was blushing a little bit, but she thankfully began to describe the first project. She said there would be several projects, but there were rotten boards on the porch flooring. She wanted to get those replaced first.

I told her there would be no charges until I had finished the project to her satisfaction. She grinned again and said, "Why ever would you say that?" I explained, "Danny had said you were picky about your work, so I want to make sure it is done to your satisfaction, before I charge you". We both laughed.

We went over to inspect some of the rotten boards. When I stepped on a few boards, I noticed they were soft. I told her the soft boards probably meant that some of the floor joists were also rotten. I said that I would inspect the entire porch to come up with an estimate. She said not to bother with the estimate because it all had to be done. She asked, "When can you start? I replied, "Is tomorrow soon enough?" She laughed as she said, "I guess that will have to do".

She then asked where I was staying. I told her I was staying at the Holiday Inn Express until I could find a place to rent. She motioned me to a chair and said, "Let's talk for a minute". She continued, "Danny said you were an engineer, but you wanted to do handyman work. I don't want to pry, but I am curious about why you would want to work at something that surely cannot pay as well as working as an engineer".

I was not sure how much I wanted to tell her. I responded, "I felt burned out from my past work. Since I am single with no family, I do not need much to get by and I wanted a slower pace".

Samantha grinned again, something she did a lot, and said "Danny wanted me to ask if you are a psychopath. Are you a psychopath?"

This question caught me off guard. I finally said "Of all the questions I would have expected to be asked in our interview, that one was not on my list. So, the short answer is 'no'. But if I were a psychopath, would you expect me to answer differently?" We both laughed. She actually had a nice smile.

I had to remind myself to focus on the interview and not her. I had not had a conversation with such an attractive lady in a long time. After a short pause in our conversation, she said, "I have something to show you. I have this 3-car garage. I only have one car. Above the garage is an apartment with a kitchen, bathroom, and living room. I haven't had time to clean it up, but I think it is livable, and as far as I know, everything works".

We walked over to the garage and up the stairs to the apartment. I was not sure if there were repairs that she expected me to recommend. When we got to the apartment, it had a huge furnished living space, a large kitchen, a bathroom, and one furnished bedroom. I looked over the rooms and said, "It doesn't look like it needs any work. Did you want to remodel the apartment, or did I miss some things that need to be repaired"?

She looked confused and then started to laugh. She said, "I mean do you think you would like to rent the apartment? You could use one of the parking spaces in the garage and use the third parking space for your tools".

I am sure I blushed and said, "This is very nice and roomy, but I think this is out of my price range".

She motioned to the couch and said let's sit down. She continued, "How about I rent it to you for $500 / month, including the garage space".

I said, "Ms. Carter that is a nice gesture, but you can get much more rent than that, and remember, I may be a psychopath".

She said, "We are friends now. My friends call me Sam. Preston, it is my job to provide counseling. I am trained to read people. I do not see you as a psychopath. Seriously, I think it would be good to have someone living here on the property. I have not had any problems yet, but a woman living alone on this much property is not the safest situation.

Danny has encouraged me to rent the apartment so that other people will occasionally be seen around here. I think it may turn out to be good for both of us".

I thought about it for a few seconds. I then said, "First, if you do not mind, I would rather call you Samantha. Samantha seems to fit you better. Second, I feel that the rent is too low. How about we reevaluate the rent in a few weeks after I get a steady income? I do not want to take advantage of you. I certainly think the space is good for me. I have to admit, I had not given thought to where to keep my handyman tools. However, I am still concerned about paying you too little rent".

She said, "Okay you can call me Sam or Samantha. We will talk about the rent later, but having you here will improve the security so you will have an uphill battle to increase the rent. By the way, we will do the rent thing on a handshake, month to month. There is no need to have a formal lease agreement".

I responded, "What if I skip out owing you rent?" She replied, "I am a counselor, I can read people. You won't skip out on me". We got up and left the apartment. She said, "I will see you tomorrow. Good night".

I left to go back to the hotel thinking this had been a great day. When I approached Smitty's Bar and Grill, I decided to stop and have a couple of beers. Danny was behind the bar, so I sat at the bar. I recounted the meeting with Samantha. I told him about the work I was going to do for her and then I mentioned that I was going to rent the garage apartment. He looked a little agitated but did not say anything.

I told him that she had said she was a counselor. I asked what type of counseling she did. Danny said she did marriage counseling, as well as, counseling children from broken homes.

When I got up to leave, Danny said, "I will keep an eye on you since you will be renting the garage apartment. Samantha is like a little sister to me". I laughed a little and said that's funny because she thought she would be safer with me there. I turned and left. On the drive to the hotel, I decided I would go to the bar next to the hotel for a few days just to keep Danny wondering what was going on.

CHAPTER 3

THE MEETING OF THE THIEVES

Four men from different backgrounds. Under normal circumstances, they would never have likely known each other. However, they all attended a seminar devoted to assisting people to achieve their retirement dreams. They all listened to the seminar speaker give advice about how to save and invest properly to achieve their retirement goals. After the speaker finished his presentation, the participants were to have dinner, followed by a question-and-answer session.

Sgt. Carson knew William Jameson because of his work with the city council on a small project in the past. Sgt. Carson, William Jameson, and two other men ended up sitting at the same dinner table and naturally had a conversation about the retirement seminar. The other two men were Father Bishop, the local Catholic priest, and Jerry Truman, the owner of the largest Mercedes dealership in Bamburg County. They seemed to all agree that the problem with the seminar was that it assumed that the participants had access to spare money and lots of time to let the investments grow.

After a few drinks, they each started sharing their original retirement goals and how they saw no way to reach those goals. All four men mentioned that they were around large sums of money. Jerry spoke up and said it was too bad that we could not siphon off a little here and there. The other three men looked at each other. William said, "What do you mean by that, Jerry"? Jerry hesitated for a few seconds and said, "We all handle a lot of money. What if we paid ourselves a small tax on the money that passes through us? We could set up our own retirement fund".

William was the first to respond, "That would not be ethical or legal". Jerry said, "Is it right that the four of us serve the public in our own jobs, and here we are approaching retirement and have almost nothing to show for it. It really gives us something to think about".

As if fate chose this time to close the subject, the seminar participants were called to reconvene for the question-and-answer session. All four men were thankful for the end of the previous discussion. But the words Jerry had spoken resonated with all four of them. As they left the seminar, the four men almost forgot all the information that the seminar speaker had presented. Their minds could not dismiss the seeds that Jerry had planted. No more was said that night about Jerry's words.

But for the next few weeks, all four men ran different scenarios through their minds. It almost seemed fitting that the least ethical of the four was the only one that could crystallize on the one thought they each had, but that was deep in their subconscious.

A few weeks later, Jerry called the other three men and proposed they get together to discuss what they had learned. All four men knew that this was not to discuss the seminar topic. The seed that Jerry had planted in their minds had germinated and was growing. They agreed to meet and decided to meet at the Pizza Hut in Brandenburg.

At the meeting, Jerry spoke up first. He began, "I propose that we 'tax' some of the money that passes through our hands and start a joint retirement fund. I have moved money around through several banks to kind of hide the money from my previous wives. I know how to do this discretely. I suggest this can be done slowly so as not to attract attention. Again, I am not suggesting that we take a large sum of money at one time, just a 'small tax'. If we do this over several years, we could end up achieving the retirement we all mentioned in the seminar during the planning session. My philosophy is that everything is not black or white. There are things that are in the gray area. I propose that we let the public fund the retirement we have earned with our service to the community".

The only response the other three had was that what Jerry said made some sense, but they would have to think about it. They did think about it for a couple of months. William called another meeting and the new retirement group settled on a plan. They figured with proper planning and carefully covering their tracks they could accomplish their goals in another two or three years. A few weeks later they met again and set the "retirement plan" in motion. For three years things worked as they had planned.

Now over three years later, Father Jonathon Bishop contacted William Jameson and asked him to contact Jerry Truman and Sgt. Jim Carson to come to a meeting at the Lazy Goat restaurant in Spencer, a neighboring town to Sandton on Monday night at 9:00. All he would tell William was that it was very urgent. The secret, unscheduled meeting came as a surprise to the other three.

They had agreed that the four of them should not meet in Sandton and meetings should only be on rare occasions. Father Bishop and William Jameson had been taking money from the church coffers and City Council funds for over three years. Sgt. Carson's job was to handle any situations that might arise if any knowledge of the missing funds were to surface. Jerry Truman's job was to take care of hiding the money in a way that could not be traced to any of them. He was familiar with these kinds of dealings and set up accounts with several banks in other towns. In addition, he ran the money through his automobile dealership, making it next to impossible to trace. The total amount of money that they had been able to steal from the Catholic Church and City Council over the last three years was almost 4 million dollars.

Father Bishop began explaining that he called this urgent meeting because a couple of men in his congregation were beginning to ask questions about funds that could be available to buy a downtown building that could be converted into an orphanage and school. While the discussions were in the initial stage, Father Bishop was afraid they would begin asking about how much money the church had and how they should go about developing a proposal for the project. To buy time, Father Bishop told them that he was tied up for a few weeks but would get back to them when he finished the project he was working on.

Father Bishop told his fellow conspirators that there was very little money in the church fund since he had "removed" over two million dollars, and he was scared. A jail cell was not how he planned to spend his retirement. He said they needed to consider returning the church's money before someone discovered that there was little money left in the church account.

The other three conspirators said with one voice, "No way !". William Jameson said, "We worked too hard to get this set up. We will have to find another way. We have covered our tracts well. Let's think through this and not act hastily. If we put our heads together, we can develop a plan".

Father Bishop jumped up and fired back, "Look, fellows, it is my head on the chopping block. You guys may be well-covered, but I am the one that will have to face the questions about the missing money. The congregation and possibly the law will demand an answer. This new development is serious!

William said, "Okay, okay. It is getting late. Let's have a couple of drinks, go home and give it some thought. We are all well respected in town. No one suspects anything, so let's keep our heads. Father Bishop, give us a few days to figure this out. Just keep your cool and don't panic. We will meet again, Saturday night, here at 7:00. Let's have a drink".

Father Bishop replied that he had to go, but he would be okay until they got together in a week or so. As he walked out, the other three looked at each other. Sgt. Carson was the first to speak up. "I told you we should not have brought him in. He is too weak, too undependable".

It was Jerry who spoke up next. "Bishop is weak, but don't forget, he is responsible for a good portion of the money we have put together. Don't get me wrong, William. The money from the city fund is significant, but Bishop has been crucial to our retirement fund.

William cleared his throat and said, "Jim, you are a policeman. What are we facing here? What are the best and worst-case scenarios?"

Sgt. Carson rubbed his chin and stared at William for several long, uncomfortable seconds. He then took a sip of his drink and began his response. "The worst-case scenario is that Bishop panics, spills his guts, and drags us down with him. He may not break immediately, but I've seen hard cases break with time. I don't think he would last long if a seasoned investigator questioned him. Bear in mind, that the investigator or prosecutor would have no reason to link us to him, but all it would take is one slip-up by Bishop. After that, our whole house of cards could come crashing down".

Jerry jumped up, spilling his drink said, "Whoa, wait a minute! Where are you going with this? I thought we were going to figure a way out of this. I may have done some questionable things in the past, but it sounds like you are putting a noose around all our necks".

William spoke up again, "Let's settle down. Jim just gave us the worst-case scenario. Let's hear the best-case scenario".

Jim continued. "I did not finish the worst-case scenario. The bottom line is what we have done is to commit fraud. That will get us 20+ years in prison. That may be bad for you guys, but for a cop to go to prison is the same as a death sentence. There are too many guys there that I helped put away. Now, that is the worst-case scenario. From the looks on your faces, I have your attention".

William said, "Jim, you have our attention. We are now in

ASSISTED SUICIDE OR MURDER?

unfamiliar territory for Jerry, Bishop and me. This is your backyard. What is the best-case scenario and what should we do now?"

Jim responded, "You are right. This falls in an area that I am all too familiar with. Bishop should not have to face an investigator or prosecutor in the best-case scenario. However, even if we were to return the money secretly, there is no assurance that Bishop would not develop a guilty conscience and spill his guts later. I need time to think about this for a few days. I will come up with a way that Bishop will avoid being questioned. Let's get back together, just the three of us on Friday. I will have some ideas by then".

These four men would never have run in the same circles or been members of the same clubs. The one fact that brought these four men together was that they all felt they deserved more out of life than they currently have. William Jameson owns a reasonably successful insurance agency. He serves on the city council and has worked his way up to the chairmanship with the ultimate goal of being the town mayor. He wanted a big house on the lake at the country club. But he did not see any of his dreams coming true in the near future.

Jerry Truman owns the largest Mercedes dealership in Bamberg County. He has been married three times and is currently divorced. Even though his dealership is large, he has not managed his money well. His three divorces have not helped in that regard. Over the years, he has become very comfortable operating in gray areas. He does not like to look at things as black and white. There always have to be some gray areas. He does not see himself as a bad person, since he is not a violent person and would not personally hurt anyone. But with the money that flows through his business, he has had enough opportunities to get himself into financial trouble by gambling and making bad investments. His three divorces are a prime example of his bad judgment in the past.

Father Bishop has been on shaky ground mentally for the last eight years. He had contemplated giving up the ministry, moving to South America, and starting a family. He had to keep all his thoughts to himself for obvious reasons and feels disoriented most of the time. Because he was so mixed up about what he should do, he had done nothing until the last three years.

Sgt. Jim Carson has been on the police force for thirty-five years and has been passed over twice for promotion to Lieutenant. His big dream was to retire, buy a large boat and move to Mexico. He knew that he did not have enough money to make his dream a reality, but he had managed to squirrel away some money. He personally handled a couple of drug busts and was able to hide away $ 45,000. He told anyone that would listen that after giving thirty-five years of his life to the police force all he would end up with is a pension of $ 2,500 per month.

That was three years ago. Now they were facing a major situation. Because of the stress of this development with Father Bishop and the guilt for what they have done, they were bordering on panic. Jim sensed their panic and told them he would have a plan together on Friday.

CHAPTER 4

A PLAN DEVELOPS

The ball was in Jim's court now. He felt that he was the only one with enough grit to do what had to be done. He also is the only one who knows the right kind of people that can do what is necessary. His big job is going to be to convince the other two of how they were going to have to handle the Bishop issue. He knew that if nothing was done, then all four of them would be facing the worst-case scenario. He could not let that happen. He was not going to prison.

He did not go into details with William and Jerry, but he knew they would likely be sent to one of the country club prisons. Since he was a policeman, the judge would treat him differently. He would probably end up in a prison with more unsavory prisoners. Seldom did a cop convicted of a serious crime like stealing from a church and the city government live through their time in prison. Between the gangs and criminals, he may have sent to prison, there was always someone that wants a piece of the cop.

His job now was to develop a plan that would keep himself, William, and Jerry out of trouble and with no suspicion of any wrongdoing. He did not mention it to William or Jerry, but he know that Bishop could not be allowed to be questioned. That meant only one thing. Bishop had to be taken out of the picture.

They could try to convince Bishop to go to South America now, to get out before anyone found out that the money was missing. That should take care of the other three. However, there was a serious risk to that option. If Bishop gets down to South America and after a while becomes disillusioned, he may decide to come back to the USA. Then it would only be a matter of time before he would be found out. The risk would then be that his actions may lead to his involvement with myself, William, and Jerry. It is just too risky. Jim had to come up with a more permanent solution.

Although the four of men had never thought they would get into a situation that they could not handle, they now were facing serious prison time. They had covered their tracks reasonably well. What they had not counted on was that Bishop might one day become the weak link in their partnership. The only sensible solution was to remove the weak link.

Getting Bishop out of the country may work for a while, but they would never have peace of mind that it would not explode on them eventually. In Jim's mind, he knew they only had one permanent solution. Jim's problem was how to handle Jerry and William. Jim knew they did not have the stomach for this kind of action. He also knew he would have to work out a story that sounds reasonable to get them to go along until it was too late for them to back out. Jim assumed He could deal with Jerry and William later, but will have to develop a foolproof plan of action that does not require them to know all the steps of the plan.

Jim thought that if he could find a way to take Bishop out in a public situation, then by the time anyone found out that the money was gone, the other three could have covered their tracks. The one thing that Jim was sure of is that the three of them cannot be directly involved in taking Bishop out. There always seem to be some mistakes that criminals make that eventually can lead the authorities back to the perpetrators. Jim thought he would have to work through a third party completely.

Jim thought he knew many guys that would be able to do the job and would be affordable. The main problem with using someone like that is that they would probably be smart enough to work out a plan in case they get caught. Jim thought that is what he would do. He would keep proof of who hired him so he could make a deal with the district attorney if he did get caught.

Jim had been thinking that he would have to arrange for Bishop to have an "accident". That is when his mind shifted to the new guy, Preston whom he has had several drinks with over the last few weeks. Preston is getting low on money, based on what he has told me. The fact that he had been a sniper may work out better than the "accident".

Jim started thinking about what could make a seemingly "honest" guy like Preston be willing to do what must be done. The more Jim thought about Preston he realized he do not think that Preston has it in himself to go through with the whole process. That is when a better plan came to his mind. He could use a second person to do the real shooting and set up enough evidence to put the blame on Preston.

Jim's main job would be to find a way to convince Preston

to go along long enough so I can generate enough evidence that would point to him. The other logistics are the location and timing to allow enough time to set up a shooting location for Preston and one for the real shooter.

The pieces of the plan were coming together. Jim realized that he needed to be careful not to let his overconfidence cause him to overlook something important. Having the potential shooters lined up in his mind was one thing, but there are numerous other details equally as important if he wants to make certain Jerry, William, and himself stay in the clear.

While thinking about the location, Jim remembered what Bishop had said about the two guys in his congregation that wanted to use a downtown building for a school and orphanage. A thought came to him. Downtown there is a vacant building on Bryant Street. It used to be a two-story office building with offices already divided up. It would not be difficult to turn it into a multipurpose school and orphanage. Because of the wooded area behind the building, most people would probably agree that it is a good location for the school and orphanage. The wooded area would provide enough green space for a playground for the school.

Across Bryant Street is Cary's General Store. The building that has been home for Cary's General story for over 40 years has a second floor that is currently vacant. It has a separate entrance in the back of the building and is not part of the store. Bishop could set up a public ceremony on the front lawn of the vacant building with Bishop giving the announcement of the upcoming project to turn the building into a school and orphanage.

Bishop could then retire to South America. Jim would have to convince Bishop that he would return the money to the church coffers following the public announcement and Bishop's retirement. Jim didn't think it will be hard to convince him to go along with this plan. Jim thought he may have to offer Bishop some money to do his South American thing, but he is so ready to change his life that he will probably jump at the chance. He will not realize just how big of a change it will be for him.

Jim thought that he and Preston could set up a sniper stand on the vacant second floor above the store. That would be where Preston would be. The real shooter would be on Cary's General's roof and would remain there until the coast was clear. In the meantime, Jim would catch Preston attempting to leave the building. Jim would then shoot him and plant a pistol on him to make it look like self-defense. Meanwhile, the real shooter would be able to escape without fear of getting caught.

This plan might just work. It has a few challenges, but it would be up to Jim to polish it up.

CHAPTER 5

WORK AT SAMANTHA'S PLACE BEGINS

I went back to Samantha's place to make a list of materials he needed to get to begin work on the porch. I also realized that I would need some basic carpenter tools. I made a list of the materials like lumber, nails, and screws. I also made a list of the tools I will need to be a real handyman.

While I was buying the tools and material for the porch, I began to feel that this may just be what I needed to get back to living. After I finished buying the materials and tools I would need, I decided to check out of the hotel and get some lunch.

When I got back to Samantha's house, I moved my stuff into the garage apartment. I thought to myself that this apartment was nicer than what I had expected to be able to rent. It was furnished nicely and had plenty of space. The garage and extra space for my tools were an extra added benefit.

For the rest of the day while measuring, sawing, and hammering I did not have any thoughts about my past life or the husbandless family back in Houston, Texas.

Samantha arrived in the late afternoon and was surprised at

how much progress I had made. I explained that some parts of the project will go faster than others. She was pleased that I had moved into the garage apartment.

She disappeared into the house and came back with a pitcher of lemonade. She said "It's time for a break" so we sat down on the porch. It was a very pleasant day with all the large trees around the house and the birds singing in the trees.

"How did you learn to do all this, Preston? Engineering school?" asked Samantha.

"Not in college. I grew up on a small farm in Texas. If my dad couldn't make it or maintain it then we didn't have it. I learned by helping my dad. He later was called back into the Army when the Kuwait war first started. He died while in Kuwait."

I saw Samantha begin to tear up so I decided to change the subject. As we drank the lemonade, I asked her how her day was saving marriages and righting wrongs in Sandton.

She laughed and said it had been a slow day. She hesitated, then said "Preston, tell me about your life before Sandton. I really don't know anything about you".

I thought for a long minute. I said, "I have not talked much about my past to anyone lately". I failed to mention the talk I had with the police sergeant. She told me to just share what I felt comfortable talking about. I decided that since I was working for her and renting her apartment, I owed her some information about my past.

I said "You are right, Samantha. I should be more open about myself since I am working for you and renting your apartment. I have a college degree in chemical engineering. Because of the war in Afghanistan, I joined the Marines. After basic training at Parris Island, I was sent to special forces training, which in the Marines is called "force recon". That stands for reconnaissance with force when needed. After a lengthy training period, I was dispatched to Afghanistan. I served in force recon for five years and then a few more assignments for two years. After eight years in the Marines, I decided I was ready to get out of the Marines.

"After leaving the Marines, I was able to find a job as a chemical engineer designing chemical plants in the southern part of the United States. I did that for about eight years and then decided to start my own engineering firm in Oklahoma City. My business was fairly successful. This is where it gets a little emotional for me. My company designed a plant in Houston, Texas.

"Everything was fine until one day I got a call from Texas. I was told that there was an explosion at the plant and that an operator had been killed.

"My number two guy and I immediately drove down to Houston to assist in the investigation. Of course, OSHA would actually perform the official investigation, but we told them we would help in any way we could. We decided to return to Oklahoma City to gather drawings and all documentation that would be needed in the investigation.

"We returned to Houston with the documentation and turned it over to OSHA. It took almost three weeks for the OSHA report to be completed and issued. It concluded that the accident was the result of the operator not following the written operating procedures.

While that cleared my company of any wrongdoing, I still

felt devastated. Don't get me wrong, my Marine experience in Afghanistan had me surrounded by death constantly, but this was different. The death in Texas was not the result of war. It was just part of regular life. I found out the operator was about 36 years old and had a wife and two young children. To make matters worse, the company only had a $ 50,000 life insurance policy for the operator's family.

Samantha sniffed and dabbed at her eyes.

"Legally, my company was not at fault and was not liable for any lawsuits. However, the whole incident literally destroyed me. Right or wrong, I felt responsible. I couldn't work or sleep. I didn't want to be around my friends, I guess because I was ashamed. It was like I blamed myself.

I can't explain why, but I knew I could not go on as if nothing had happened. After three or four weeks of sleepless nights, and not being able to face friends, I decided I had to make a change. I sold my house and business and cashed in my 401 K account. I had about $ 950,000. I kept out $ 50,000 and arranged for the operator's family to have the rest. I had to leave Oklahoma City. I ended up here in Sandton".

I looked at Samantha and saw she had teared up, just as I had. She said, "But you were not guilty. You were very generous. Most people would have done nothing."

I said " Samantha, I have not opened up like this to anyone else. You must be a good counselor ".

She smiled and said "All I did was listen to you. You just let things out that needed to come out. You cannot carry around a weight that is not yours to carry. You did nothing wrong. In fact, what you did for that family is commendable. It will take time, but you have to find a way to forgive yourself. I think it is time for something stronger than lemonade".

We each had a beer and just sat there for a while without many conversations. I finally said, " I should not have burdened you with that long story, but I have to admit I had felt uncomfortable not telling you about my past. Now that the whole story is out, we may need to revisit the question of psychopath".

Samantha said, "You are anything but a psychopath. You get a good night's sleep and get back to work on my house. This subject will only come up again if you would like to discuss it further in a counseling session, for which there will be no charge. Good night, see you tomorrow".

CHAPTER 6

SGT. CARSON FINDS PRESTON

Sgt. Carson ordered another beer at the bar where he first met Preston Bourne. Just another night at the bar. Sgt. Carson has been at the bar for the last two nights hoping to meet Preston. It was time to put the plan into action. He thought, right now, I wish I had some of my brother-in-law's sales pitch abilities. I have to convince a seemingly honest guy to shoot someone he does not know. I was pretty sure that I need to ease into the part of the plan that includes shooting someone. Just thinking about that convinces me that I do not have a snowball chance in hell of pulling this off.

As I was beginning to doubt the whole idea of using Preston to take out Bishop, Preston walked into the bar. I caught his eye and waved him over. I decided that at least three or more beers would be required before I could start any discussion about Bishop.

Preston began with "We are going to have to stop meeting like this".

Jim responded, "What else do two old bachelors have to do but drink and tell old war stories. I guess, in your case, it would be real war stories. Was that a pun? I never understood what exactly a pun was".

Preston said we could just stick to drinking, and he ordered a beer. As we drank, Jim asked Preston how things were going. Preston said things were about the same and that he was doing a small porch repair job.

"That should help with your finances.

Preston said, "I am not hurting but did need to find something soon or consider moving somewhere else. I will give it another couple of months before I do anything drastic".

Jim said, "Don't worry. Something will turn up. "I have an idea that might develop soon. Preston, I am curious about your time in the service. You said you were a Marine sniper. Did it take a lot of training?"

Preston responded, "The training time depended on several factors, including past experience with firearms. More important was the current demand for snipers and what was going on with the military around the world. When military things heat up, politicians would start screaming for soldiers in the field without regard to what training they had or didn't have."

Preston said, "My training was for approximately one year. Normally you trained with a spotter after your initial training on the shooting range. Working with a spotter could then take several months to get comfortable with each other. The reason it sometimes takes so long to get to the point that you trust each other is because your life is on the line. Also, since some assignments may require you to be in place for hours doing nothing except waiting and watching, your temperaments and patience levels must be compatible".

Jim said, "Preston, you do not seem like a very aggressive individual, and I deal with aggressive people all the time. What made you choose to go into being a sniper? I do not mean to pry, but it is interesting to me, especially with the business I am in. If you do not mind, I would love to better understand the sniper thought process".

We ordered another beer and Preston said, "I do not mind talking about it. I am not an aggressive person at all. I do believe though that there is a need for snipers during war times, fundamentally, to make it safer for other troops. We were at war, after all. I may take one life to save hundreds of soldiers. I had known snipers that did not have a good understanding of that basic fact. It eventually sent them over the hill, so to speak. They would wash out of the service after only a few assignments".

Preston said, "Don't get me wrong. There are some snipers that have an aggressive attitude or personality. They just seem to enjoy what they are doing, primarily for the rush of the moment. I, however, believed in what I was doing and was good at my job. After a while though, even the toughest snipers either die or just quit. I was fortunate and knew when it was time for me to quit. Some of my assignments began to seem more like personal vendettas than military operations. That was when I decided to hang it up".

"Preston, I just have to ask. How do you justify killing someone? I have on occasion been around someone that has killed somebody, and they always seem to justify it for one reason or another. If you are out on an assignment and they are shooting at you, I can understand. But to lay in wait to shoot someone seems different."

Preston thought for a few seconds and responded. "As I said before, it comes down to taking one life to save multiple others. I am not sure I can give more justification than that. In your own job, if you have to shoot someone that is endangering other people, do you feel justified in that situation?"

Jim responded, "Yes, I guess I understand what you are saying. Do you think about the people you killed, have nightmares or anything like that?"

Preston responded, "Generally, all I knew about my targets was that they were enemies at war. I didn't know if they had families or anything about them. No, I guess I just put them in a locked room in my brain".

We drank another beer and Jim said, "Preston, I have a matter I would like to talk to you about, but I would rather it be in a quieter and more private place. Would you mind us meeting tomorrow night and continuing our drinking and conversation at my apartment?" Preston agreed and we decided to call it a night, settled up at the bar, and left.

The next night Jim told Preston that he may have some work, and if it did come about, Preston would be able to stay in Sandton for a while. Jim told him it was really a nice, quiet town. We got a couple of beers and talked in general about Sandton and how the area was growing. By the time we finished our second beer, we were done with our chit-chat. Jim asked Preston if he wanted something stronger, but we agreed to stick to beer.

Jim said, "I want to tell you a story and why I may have some work for you. Sandton has a Catholic church, and the priest is Father Bishop. He has been in Sandton for ten or twelve years. We became good friends, even though I am not Catholic. He recently discovered that he has cancer. I am not sure what type, but it is serious. The treatments are very expensive, and he was not sure what to do about them. In a weak moment, he took money from the church's bank account. He figured that when the treatments were over, he would replace the money over the next year or two.

"Unfortunately, the treatments took longer than he expected and therefore required more and more money. The bottom line, without realizing it, he ended up taking over one million dollars out of the church account. His original plan was that it would only take maybe fifty thousand and he could repay that. He definitely intended to return the money. However, when the cost kept adding up, he panicked. He knew he could never come up with that much money.

"He came to me for advice, but I had no idea what to tell him. He told me he had taken out a life insurance policy last year for two million dollars. He originally planned to set up his will to fund several charities.

"To add to his predicament, two guys in his congregation came up with an idea to start up a church school and orphanage with church money. He agreed with them that it sounded like a good idea. However, after the last treatment, the doctors explained that the treatments did not do any good and that his case was terminal. The doctors said the prognosis was two months or three at most.

"After getting over the shock of what the doctors had said, he realized that the life insurance policy could replace the church money. He asked me to assist him in getting the money back into the church account after he died. He said he would make me the beneficiary of the policy. However, since he had already been diagnosed with cancer, he was afraid that the policy would not cover pre-existing cancer during the first two years of the policy.

"He was really panicked now. He realized that he may not be able to stall the two guys that wanted to set up the school and orphanage. He said that even though the doctors told him the prognosis was two or three months, what if it went longer?

"Father Bishop could not stand the fact that he had taken money from the church and the effect it would have on his parishioners when they found out what he had done. He pleaded with me to help him come up with a solution. He asked me if I could arrange an "accident" that would end his life mercifully and quickly since he was dying anyway. He said that I could then replace the money in the church's account from the life insurance and avoid him spending his last days facing the shame of what he had done being made public or worse, dying in jail".

I explain, "Sgt. Carson, what you are asking is very risky. Insurance investigators often suspect staged "accidents", especially on large life insurance policies. Even the best staged "accidents" often have one or two simple mistakes. That is all it takes for the insurance companies to deny payment. A staged "accident" would be treated as a suicide and not covered by his policy".

"Preston, I think the reason I wanted to talk to you privately is clear now. This kind of conversation would spoil everything that Father Bishop wanted to do if anyone overheard it".

"Sgt. Carson, I am puzzled why you told me all this. While I would not have any reason to tell anyone, it is still a chance you are taking by you sharing this with me. Why would you do that"?

"Preston, when you mentioned that you were a sniper, I thought you might be able to help me. Father Bishop only has two months to live and most of that time will be with suffering. This is why Father Bishop was asking me to help him basically to die mercifully and to avoid the damage to the church when they find out the money is gone and that he essentially stole it".

"Sgt. Carson, are you asking me to murder a Catholic priest? While I understand the circumstances, people who commit murder still go to jail or are put to death in South Carolina. I am not a murderer. There is a major difference between a hit man and a sniper in the armed forces. You may not understand the difference, but they are not the same".

"I know Preston, but this is essentially an "assisted suicide". I would just like you to think about it. I talked to Father Bishop about you without mentioning your name. He was excited. He has really been despondent about his situation. Not about dying, but about the money he took. He said "assisted suicide" was the best solution, all things considered.

Since his cancer is terminal, he did not want to go through the pain from cancer and the humiliation of being found out to have taken church money. He wanted to have this handled soon, so the life insurance would have time to pay off the policy and the money returned to the church account before the church started looking for the money for the project.

Jim said, "He actually set up an account in another town and moved the church money there, supposedly so local people would not gossip about how much money the church had. It was really so the money could be replaced with no one in Sandton knowing about it. I know it did not make good sense, but he has been under a lot of stress and not thinking too clearly. Since we have been talking about possible ways out of this mess, he has settled down and seems to be relieved of the stress.

"Preston, this is a lot to drop on you all of a sudden. I don't expect you to make a decision tonight, although Father Bishop is anxious to set this in motion. Father Bishop did say that he felt it only proper to give you some expense money, to cover the cost of you taking time off to go away for a few weeks. He wondered if $ 50,000 was enough. Understand, this is not money to kill someone, it is to give you the money to take a vacation until this excitement blows over. I don't expect an answer now, just think about it".

I said, "Sgt. Carson, this is a lot to take in. I have never had to make this kind of decision. I would like to meet with Father Bishop, not to talk about the actual incident, but just to get a better feeling about him".

Jim said he did not think that would be possible. He and Father Bishop had discussed that but did not think that was wise. If the two of you were ever seen together, that would ruin the insurance payment. Sgt. Carson seemed a little nervous about my suggestion.

Jim said, "Father Bishop and I talked about how to arrange the event. He told me that the two guys that wanted to build the school and orphanage thought downtown Sandton was a great location. I found a good place downtown to make the announcement. The site also had a good location for a sniper's hideout. Is that what you call it?" Preston said, "Some people do Jim, but it is usually just referred to as a sniper's nest".

Jim said, "The place that Father Bishop and I found for the school and orphanage is a vacant building on Bryant Street. It is a large two-story building with offices that can be converted into bedrooms or classrooms. It has a wooded area behind the building that would function as a play area for the school. Father Bishop said he could make a public announcement on the front steps of the building about the church developing the property into a school and orphanage. Across the street is a two-story building. The ground floor is occupied by Cary's General Store. The second floor is vacant and has a separate back entrance.

"I thought I could leave a navy-blue Honda Accord on a side street for you to take to Summerville immediately after the assisted suicide. Summerville is over an hour away, normally. With fast driving, you could be there in around 45 minutes. We can arrange to have a realtor show you some places to rent, just to establish an alibi.

"I do not think you would even need an alibi, but it is just a precaution. I can arrange a manhunt in the opposite direction, by saying I saw someone running away in that direction. I have had time to think about this and I am sure I can steer the search for the shooter in the opposite direction. I can give a description of the "shooter" as a middle-aged man dressed like a biker. In the meantime, you will be gone in the opposite direction looking at rent houses. I just want you to think about it. Sleep on it and we can get together in the next few days here at my apartment. We can cover any questions you may have then".

Preston said, " Sgt. Carson, I can understand you are close to this Father Bishop, and I even understand why you may have thought of me. Why would you not just arrange some kind of accident? Your plan is very complicated and even strange. It seems you could arrange an accident with no one else involved. It would be less risky".

Preston, I am just afraid that because of my friendship with Father Bishop, some people might get suspicious, especially if word got out about the life insurance proceeds being left to me. I think the best thing would be a public event with me there with him, or at least close by".

"I guess I see that, Sgt. Carson. It still feels strange. Let me think about it. I will meet you in a couple of days".

CHAPTER 7

WORK AT SAMANTHA'S PLACE

Having made good progress on Samantha's porch on the first day, I started work on replacing all the rotted floor joists. Even though I was having trouble concentrating because of last night's conversation with Sgt. Carson, I was able to finish all the carpentry work on the porch. Luckily, there was only about one-third of the floor joists that need to be repaired. After finishing the carpentry work, I decided to put the first coat of paint on the raw wood that I had installed. I would have to talk to Samantha about whether she wanted the whole porch painted.

I walked around the outside of the house. It really was a grand house. Fixed up it would be an outstanding house in the neighborhood. I found a few facia boards near the roof that needed to be replaced and a few of the window casings that needed to be replaced.

When Samantha arrived, I had just finished my walk-around inspection. I suggested we sit on the porch and have some of her good lemonade after she got settled in to discuss the future work.

While drinking our lemonade, I told her that I had moved into the apartment. She seemed pleased that I had moved in and said to let her know if I needed anything.

I told her that the carpentry work on the porch was finished and that I had put a prime coat of paint on the raw wood I had installed. I asked her whether she wanted the whole porch repainted. She asked my opinion and I said we should repaint the whole porch and ceiling so that everything would match and look new. That settled, I mentioned that there were some facia boards that needed replacing and that it was not a big job.

The next question was about the window casings that were rotten. She said not to bother with replacing the casings, she just wanted to replace all the windows because they were older windows and she wanted new, double pane windows that were easy to open. I told her that she had about thirty windows and that would be around $ 12,000. She said that we would discuss that later because she was thinking about rearranging some rooms.

I said, " With the facia board work and painting the porch, I have enough to keep me busy for a while. We can talk about what other projects you have in mind". I was beginning to be afraid that she might not understand how much her projects would cost, and I did not want her to run out of money.

Samantha spoke up and said, "Enough talk about remodeling, I have a surprise. I am going to fix us dinner tonight, if you do not have other plans".

I said that I had no plans, but didn't want to be much trouble, and I would be glad to pick up something for us. She said no, she wanted to prepare dinner. She asked if a salad, chicken and rice, and apple pie for dessert would be okay. I, of course, said that sounded great. We decided that we would eat at 7:00, so I went back to my apartment to get cleaned up for dinner.

When I returned to her house, the aroma of baked chicken and rice, with hints of apple and cinnamon greeted me. Samantha told me to come in and make myself comfortable. She asked if I would like a glass of wine and I responded that I would like a white wine to go with the chicken. She brought our wine into the den. She was dressed casually in blue jeans and a white shirt but was absolutely beautiful. I raised my wine glass. "Here's to you. You put the models in the magazines to shame."

She blushed and said, "That earned you a second dessert." She tinked her wine glass to mine.

I tilted my head toward the kitchen. "I have not had a home-cooked meal in years, not counting what I cooked.

We finished our wine, and Samantha excused herself to go back to the kitchen. She returned after a few minutes and led me into her dining room. She furnished it simply but elegantly with two candles on the oaken table with our dinner between them. I pulled out my chair and put it beside her chair instead of sitting opposite her.

Her chicken cooked with white rice, dribbled with a light cream gravy and finely chopped green onions looked and smelled wonderful. I have never had chicken and rice, but it was my new favorite meal.

With the salad, chicken and rice, and the apple pie dessert, I said I would have to take a raincheck on the second dessert. I knew it would most likely be here tomorrow for our afternoon snack. We sat and talked for quite a while. It seemed like we never ran out of things to talk about.

When the conversation began to slow down, I said it was time to clean up the dishes and kitchen. She of course said not to worry she would take care of it.

I said no, the meal was so good, that I would not let her have to do all the clean-up by herself. The first question was who was going to wash and who would dry. I said I was better at washing and also did not know where the dishes should go after drying so that settled it.

As we were finishing putting things away, we turned around and were face to face. I am not sure what came over me, but I kissed her on her lips with a short kiss. I raised up stunned but then said, "What the heck" and kissed her again, but this time a much deeper kiss. And she was kissing back.

When we parted, I said, "I am sorry, I do not know what came over me".

She said "The same thing that came over me. If you are not sure what it was that came over you, we can try again to see if we can figure it out".

We both started laughing and decided to have another glass of wine and return to the couch. While we were drinking our wine, I said, "This has been the best day of my life. I am serious, I moved into my great apartment, had the best home-cooked meal ever, and then you know the rest".

Samantha said, "It is strange that you would say that. That was exactly the same thought that was going through my head, down to the last minute of it. Tonight has set the bar very high".

This time it was me grinning. I said, " I accept the challenge. Tomorrow night I want to take you out to eat. I am not sure how to have a night better than tonight, but I am willing to try". I pulled her to me, and we just sat there with my arms around her. We did not need to talk. We just savored the moments.

After a while, I said, "Are you this nice to all your handymen?"

Samantha said, "Yes, since you are the only handyman I have ever had, I would have to say this is my handyman treatment. What I want to know is how you plan on improving on tonight".

The only response I had was "Just wear your best dress tomorrow night, and we will go out. I am not saying that any meal we can get will be as good as what you served tonight, but we can practice on the kissing part".

We agreed on me picking her up at 6:30 because I told her we were going to go the Brandenburg which was 45 minutes away.

My head was spinning the next day. I tried to get some work done, but I was trying to figure out what was happening. This was an area I had never been in. Could something like what I thought was going on happen this quickly? Since this was new territory for me, I decided to keep moving forward and not try to figure things out, just let them happen.

When I walked over to Samantha's house and knocked on the door, she said to come in. When I opened the door, she was standing there in a black dress. I was speechless for what seemed like an eternity. Finally, I said, "You are beautiful. What are you doing going out in public with a guy like me?"

She said, "Don't be silly. We will likely be the couple of the year. Do you know, this is the first time anyone has said I am beautiful?"

I responded, "I find that hard to believe, but I can guarantee you that this will not be the last time you will hear it".

She said, "Where are we going tonight?"

I said, "I did some research in Brandenburg and found that the best restaurant in town is the Silver Slipper. Have you ever been there?"

Samantha said, "No, that restaurant has been a little too expensive for me. Are you sure you can afford it and what is the occasion?"

I said, "Remember, we set the bar high last night. And as far as the expense, I work for a high-class lady. She is loaded and does not watch what I charge her".

Samantha said, "You haven't been flirting with your high-class lady have you? I would hate to think that I was going out tonight with a gigolo". In the most serious voice, I could come up with, I said, "I am afraid that it has gone beyond flirting, but let's change the subject before I dig the hole any deeper".

I took her hand and we walked to my F-150 truck. "I hope you don't mind going in my truck. At least it is clean and dependable."

Samantha said, "With you driving, it looks like a limo."

We arrived at the restaurant and were met by a valet. I whispered, that I did not think this would be a fast-food place. When we got inside, the restaurant was the most impressive restaurant I had ever been in. I had been to some nice restaurants in Houston, but nothing like this. Each dining table had its own room-like walled enclosure on three sides for privacy. The walls were covered by expensive oil paintings. Of course, the tables had fine linen tablecloths.

After we had taken the surroundings in, the server walked over, gave us our menus, and asked what we wanted to drink. We both got a glass of wine, red for me and white for Samantha. I decided on the filet mignon and Samantha decided on the filet of sole. When the server returned, we said we would like a salad, and the filet mignon and filet of sole. After the food arrived, we noticed that when our wine drinks got low or we finished the salads, the server appeared immediately. There was no hovering or asking us anything, he just seemed to know what and when things were needed.

After we finished our salad and the main course, the server asked if we would like a dessert, and both of us said we would like a crème brulee' at the same time. The server just smiled and left. I said that it was cool that we liked the same desserts. She knew I was referring to last night and smiled. The meal was somewhat expensive, but we felt it was worth every cent.

The 45-minute ride home discussion was to relive the night. I told her again how absolutely beautiful she was, and we talked about making the restaurant an annual thing. I said, "You do realize we have barely known each other one week".

Samantha said, "And what is your point?"

We laughed as we drove into the driveway. Samantha said, "Do you want to come in for a glass of wine?" I said, "We could also have some more dessert". We barely made it in the door before embracing. The dessert was better that the crème brulee'.

CHAPTER 8

THE CONSUMMATION OF THE PLAN

The next day I called Sgt. Carson and we decided to meet at his apartment at 8:00. I told Samantha that I had to meet a guy about future work, and I would see her later, if our meeting did not go on too long. I began to realize that I had not been totally honest with Samantha and that felt unnerving. I was beginning to wonder why I was still talking to Sgt. Carson about his proposed work. I decided I had to tell Samantha everything, and even get her input. I was not sure about how she would react to me even considering doing the "assisted suicide". I was going to have to think long and hard about how and what I told her.

When I arrived at Sgt. Carson's apartment, I said, "Do you have any idea how weird it is to be talking with a police officer about shooting a Catholic Priest? It almost seems like I should check you for a camera or wires to see if this is a setup".

Sgt. Carson laughed. He said, "I know this is strange, Preston. In my thirty-five years on the police force, I have never been in a situation like this. You have to remember that I approached you. I have a lot at stake in this whole operation. While I am not a

Catholic, I developed a close friendship with Father Bishop. If he had not developed cancer and had taken the church money, I would have just told him he had made the bed and he had to sleep in it. I would still have tried to help him through the legal process, but definitely would not be contemplating anything like this. The cancer changed my whole way of thinking. If the treatment had worked, I would have done my best to help him find a way to repay the money. But that was not to be.

I said, " Sgt. Carson, I understand all that. Before I agree to your plan, there are a few things my training requires me to check out. First, I want to see the shooting zone. I need to check out the back entrance to the second floor above Cary's store. I need to check the line of sight from the second floor to the area where Father Bishop will be. Second, I would like to talk to Father Bishop. Not as the shooter, but just to meet him and get a sense of his mental state.

Preston, as far as your first point, no problem. I can arrange that without raising any suspicions. The second point is one that Father Bishop and I discussed. He asked my opinion and to be honest, I was against it. We both felt that any contact between the two of you could be the one mistake that may sink the whole ship. If someone happened to see you two together, and he ends up being shot, then it could draw you into the investigation. This is especially true because you are new to this area. And also, if anyone found out that you were a past Marine sniper, that would be disastrous. The more we talked about it the more he was convinced he did not want to take the chance".

Okay Sgt. I'll give on point 2. One question about your plan.

After the shot, if I take the money and go away, will that throw me under suspicion? I do not want to be constantly looking over my shoulder. There is also a third point. I think the fee should be $ 100,000 with $ 50,000 up front and the remainder after it is completed.

Preston, if we stick to the plan, I can make certain that we are looking for the person I say I saw running away. After all, it is in my best interest for you to be above suspicion. It will be easy for me to steer the investigation in the direction I want it to go. As far as the fee, I don't think your proposal is unreasonable, and I understand you need to lay low for a while and that will cost money. The amount we have to put back in the church account is just under two million, so it should not be a problem. Father Bishop and I discussed the remainder of the two million life insurance policy. He set up a savings account and I will put the remainder of the insurance money in that account. His will can direct the savings account to be given to the church to fund the school and orphanage.

Sgt., I need to evaluate the sniper's nest. Can you set that up for tomorrow? I will want to check the location of the sun during the day and the projected wind direction and speed. I will walk around Cary's store tomorrow morning. Will tomorrow afternoon work for looking at the second floor?

Sgt. Carson said, "Preston, I will call you tomorrow around 1:00 pm to set up a time". I immediately said, "No, Sgt., no phone records. I'll be around the back entrance at 3:00 pm. If that doesn't work for you, don't show up. We will try again at 6:00 pm. I will see you at 3:00 or 6:00 tomorrow".

As I left Sgt. Carson's apartment, I felt the adrenalin rush or excitement that I had not felt since Afghanistan. But there was something else in the background. I had a feeling that something was not right. I had that feeling when we first started talking about my involvement in this. That is why I used my thumb drive recorder for our meeting today. It was small enough to not be noticed and just looked like a standard thumb drive. I had to make sure to identify him on the recording and get his responses to my questions. A little insurance never hurts.

While I could not use the recording to clear me of my part in the plan, I could at least use it to keep Sgt. Carson from leaving me out in the cold. I was beginning to question my decision to move to Sandton and being part of this whole scheme. This was not the peace and quiet I was looking for. What I did not realize was that the peace and quiet I have with Samantha is what I had been missing. What if I mess that up?

I wondered if there was any way I could check up on Bishop's doctor's report. I am not sure of where I stand on "assisted suicide", but I do understand not wanting to go through the final stages of cancer. While I had never experienced the guilt of stealing money and the fear of getting caught, I can imagine the burden it must be, especially having taken the money from the church.

If I could see the doctor's report and confirm the life insurance policy was in place, it would go a long way to relieve the questions in the back of my mind. It just seems like Sgt. Carson could come up with a fool-proof accident that would be much simpler than this elaborate plan.

Then the thought of Samantha jumped into my mind. What

am I doing even contemplating being involved in this? I could be risking the best thing that had ever happened to me with the best person I had ever known. There was another thing bothering me. With my background, was I kidding myself that Samantha and I could have a future together? I could see this whole thing blowing up in my face tomorrow. I did not know if I were a bigger idiot thinking about getting involved in this Sgt. Carson thing or for thinking that Samantha and I could have a life together. I figured this would be a sleepless night.

CHAPTER 9

THE MEETING WITH SAMANTHA

When I drove into the driveway, I noticed that Samantha's lights were still on. I decided to get it over with tonight. I went to her door and knocked. She came to the door and smiled. I guess she saw the look on my face and asked if anything was wrong. I said, "How long do you have to talk". Samantha said, "I have a lifetime to talk. Come in and sit down, I think we may need a glass of wine".

When she came back with the wine, I told her that I had a lot of things I wanted to tell her and that she could stop me and ask questions when she wanted. I warned her that it was a long story and that I would hope that she would agree to hear it all before stopping me.

I started with, "I said I was in the Marine special forces, which was true. What I did not say was that I was a sniper in Afghanistan. I hope that does not automatically make me a psychopath".

Samantha stopped me there and said that her dad was a special forces Army soldier. She understood the need for special forces and that she did not have any problem with me being a sniper in the Marines.

I said that I appreciated that, but there is much more to the story. I continued. I told her that when I got to Sandton that I had met a police sergeant in the bar one night. I said that I had been drinking too much and I told him my life story. I told him about my time in the Marines and about being a sniper. He seemed very interested about me being a sniper. He asked a lot of questions about how snipers could justify shooting people and those types of questions. He closed out that night saying that he may have some work for me but would not know for a few weeks. I was interested in the potential future work.

I had not met you at that time and had no idea of how much handyman work you might have for me. I also had no idea that someone other than me would enter into the decision-making process. I saw that Samantha had a puzzled look on her face, so I asked if she had any questions.

Samantha asked, "What do you mean that someone else would enter the decision process?"

I said, " I thought it was obvious that I meant you. I know it is crazy since we have only known each other for a few days. You became an integral part of my life the first time we met. Before, I had no one to worry about what they might think, but now what you think of me is crowding out all my other thoughts. What you think about me is the only important thing to me.

Samantha teared up and said that she does not think she could ever think ill of me. She said I should continue and that we will discuss the details when I am finished.

I said, "The next time I ran into him at the bar he started asking me about my training as a sniper. He said that I did not seem like an aggressive person and wanted to know why I chose to be a sniper. He asked how I could justify killing a person that was not shooting at me. I went through the thought process that by killing one person, I would likely be saving tens or even hundreds of our soldiers. He agreed and said it was the same in police work.

The next night he wanted to talk to me but suggested that we meet at his apartment. He told me about the Catholic priest that he had become friends with. He said that the priest had found out that he had terminal cancer. He needed some money for his cancer treatments, so he took some money from the church account since he was in charge of handling the money. He said that he thought he could return the money to the church after he completed his treatments. One treatment led to others, so he had to take more money. In a short time, he had taken about one million dollars. This is the point that the priest told Sgt. Carson what he had done and asked for help to figure out what to do. But the next time they got together, the priest said that he had met with his doctor and was informed that his treatments had not worked, and that the cancer was terminal. The doctor told him that he only had two or three months to live.

The priest was understandably frightened. He then said that a year before he was diagnosed with cancer, he had taken out a life insurance policy for two million dollars. He knew the insurance money could replace the money he had taken, but the church would probably find out. He was worried about someone finding out about him taking the money before he died and could replace the money.

He and Sgt. Carson worked out a plan that the priest would change the beneficiary to Sgt. Carson. After the priest died, he could put the money back I the church's account. That all seemed like a reasonable plan, but the priest was worried about how much he would suffer with the cancer. And what if the cancer lasted longer than the doctor had thought.

The priest then dropped the latest disaster on Sgt. Carson. Two men from the church congregation wanted to start a church boarding school. They said that the church surely had enough money to do that and that there was a real need in Sandton. The priest said he agreed and that they would form a committee to work out the details. This now put a timetable on the whole matter.

Sgt. Carson said that the priest asked him about an "assisted suicide" or the possibility of an "accident". He was afraid that the insurance policy would not pay off for a regular suicide. Sgt. Carson told him that the both of them should think about what to do for a few days. Sgt. Carson said that was a few days before we first met and that our discussion had started him thinking. He said that he knew that I needed some work and that my work as a sniper had trained me to accept death.

He asked me what my thoughts about "assisted suicide", especially in cases of terminal illness. In the case of the priest, this would not only give him the chance to avoid a painful time before the cancer took its toll, but it would allow the church to be repaid. It would also spare the priest of the humiliation of being found out to have taken money from the church.

I will be honest with you Samantha. I did not know what I thought about an "assisted suicide" in cases with terminal illnesses. The additional thought of the priest's life work being clouded by being found out to have stolen from the church. It could be that having been a sniper and involved in death as often as I had may have confused my thinking.

Samantha looked up into my eyes and said that if she had not had a father in the Army special forces, she may not have been able to understand. She continued while still looking into my eyes, " I know you Preston and I can understand your confusion. I also know that you are a good man. The only thing I worry about is how you are handling your feelings about the operator in the plant that exploded. I wonder if you could ever come to grips with this situation, no matter which direction you take".

Samantha said, "My feelings for you have not changed in the least. If you will accept my help, I would like to work through this with you. What do you think? I would suggest that we sleep on this and talk tomorrow. I do not have anything scheduled and I am going to give my handyman the day off, so we will have all day to talk through this".

I agreed as a tear rolled down my face. She hugged me for a long time. As strange as it may sound, I felt that everything was going to work out. I had no idea of how, but just that it would. I looked into her eyes, and we kissed again. It is best to finish out the night with dessert.

Sleep was very hard that night. I am sure I slept some, but I was wide awake at 5:00 o'clock. I wondered what I would do until Samantha was ready to begin the day. The next minute, she knocked on my door. When I opened the door, she was standing there with a platter of breakfast for the two of us. I tried to break some of the tension and said, "What a wonderful way to start the day. I am new at this handyman thing. Do we do this every morning?" Samantha grinned and said, "Is that a proposal? We really have not known each other long enough for a proposal. What would people think?"

I blushed and we ate our breakfast. It was good, but we were both ready to get started.

I told Samantha that I had mentioned meeting with the priest just to get a feel for how likely he could go through with this. Sgt. Carson seemed nervous. I cannot explain, but I just felt that it was odd that he was so quick to say no to me meeting with Father Bishop.

I also went into detail about Sgt. Carson offering me $ 50,000 to carry out the "assisted suicide" and that I had said that I thought the fee should be $ 100,000. I told Samantha that I did this to see if Sgt. Carson and the priest were really serious about going through this. I also told Sgt. Carson that I had a concern about the investigation. Since I was new in town, it would be easy for my name to come up. He was quick to say that it would be easy for him to direct the investigation in another direction. He could say that he hurried over to the shooter's location and saw someone running away. He could give a description of someone that looked nothing like me. He said the money would give me a chance to lay low for a while.

Samantha, what if this is a set up to put the blame on me? I mean, an unemployed, new guy in town that just happens to be a past Marine sniper. What defense could I put up. My word against a 35-year police sergeant that has lived his whole life in Sandton. Furthermore, what if he decided to just shoot me and say he began to ask me questions and I pulled a gun and he had to shoot me.

Samantha said, "This is beginning to sound too plausible. What about this? Suppose that you tell him that you cannot go through with this. What would he likely do?"

I said, "My engineering mind is beginning to think we need to be more organized in our approach to this. I am sorry I got you into this and it makes me think I may be putting you in danger. We have to consider that. Let's write down all the options we can come up with so we can address each one completely".

I got up and found a note pad. Samantha said she would take notes. I started with Option 1.

Option 1. I go ahead and help the priest with the "assisted suicide"

Option 2. I tell Sgt. Carson that I cannot go through with this

Option 3. I go along for a while to see if I can determine if this is a set-up to blame me

Option 4. I go along for a while and then tell Sgt. Carson that I cannot go through with this

Option 5. I go to the police with this now

Option 6. I go along with this for a while then go to the police

We agreed that these seemed like the most obvious options. We figured we could add others later if needed. Samantha said, "I think we both should address each option so that we get both of our ideas out in the open. No hidden agendas, just open opinions. We can then sort out the path forward for each option. Hopefully, as we go through this process, the best path forward will begin to become clear. What do you think?"

I said, " I think you are brilliant, and I agree. Since I am the one with my finger on the trigger, so to speak, let me go first, then you follow. I also suggest we write down our ideas on each option and not try to evaluate the options until we have gone through all of them. Samantha, I really care about you and appreciate what you are trying to do. However, if it becomes apparent that I am putting you in danger, we have to agree for you to back away". Samantha shook her head and said, "It is too early to talk about that, so let's concentrate on what is in front of us".

I agreed and began, "Option 1 – I see two major concerns about Option 1. First is the question of whether Sgt. Carson is telling me the whole and honest story. The fact that he does not want me to talk to the priest seems like a red flag, but maybe not. I do not have anything to base my concern on, other than my gut feeling that something does not seem right. The second concern is whether I really think that "assisted suicide" is right and whether or not it would apply in this case".

What are your thoughts, Samantha?

She said, " I agree with both of your concerns. The fact that you are not allowed to talk to the priest does not allow you to evaluate his temperament, and it also means that you cannot verify that he has insurance that will pay out the benefit.

The second thing is honestly a larger concern to me. The tenderness you had for the operator's family indicates to me that whatever your thoughts about "assisted suicide" are now could change later. That could develop into a deep-rooted guilt. We can visit that after we go through the other options".

I now shifted to Option 2. I think the only way I could effectively tell Sgt. Carson that I was not going ahead with the "assisted suicide" was to convince him that I did not think that "assisted suicide" was right under any circumstances. I think I could make a strong argument for that position, especially since I am currently unsure that it is right or that I could go through with it.

The other thought I have about this option is that if he decides to go ahead with the "assisted suicide", he will have to find someone else to do it. He would know that I was still around knowing about the whole operation. That would be a risk for him personally. That leads into the next concern about Option 2. What if he decides to try to pin the shooting on me? On the surface, it looks like his case would be circumstantial, but he may be able to create evidence.

My last thought about Option 2 is that he and the priest could decide not to go forward and drop the whole project. What are your thoughts Samantha?

Samantha said, "Since I have no first-hand information from having talked to Sgt. Carson it is hard to form a strong opinion about Option 2. The fact that he was so quick to bring you in on the process is somewhat of an alarm or a red flag as you say. It does seem like they would probably not give up on going ahead. Of course, I have no idea how they would proceed without you.

"My first reaction would be that if they decided to go ahead, then pinning it on you would be the most logical path. That would put Sgt. Carson in the clear, that is, if he executed you. It would also take pressure off investigating who really did the shooting. If he did not execute you, you would always be a risk to him". Since Samantha paused, I assumed she was finished, so I went on the Option 3.

Option 3 assumes I make no changes in my dealings with Sgt. Carson for now. I continue meeting with him and basically go through the motions as if I am planning to go forward. The thing that this will do is give me time to watch and listen to Sgt. Carson to see if any more red flags show up. I would have to be sure I do all the expected things that a shooter would do, such as talk about the timing, visit the shooting location, discuss the get-a-way plan and finally the payment plan. What about your thoughts, Samantha?

Samantha said, "I certainly do not know anything about planning an operation to shoot someone. All the preparations sound reasonable. Would you have to worry about being seen while doing the scoping things? Do you think you will be putting yourself in more danger?"

I responded that I felt like the scoping exercise could be handled without too much exposure. As far as the danger, I did not think that Option 3 was exposing me to any more danger, and it may even be less that the other options.

Option 4 looks like a combination of Options 2 and 3. The only difference is that Option 3 shortens the schedule because of staying with the program with the endpoint staying the same. I feel the points from both Option 2 and 3 would still apply. Do you agree, Samantha?

Samantha said, " I agree that I do not see that Option 4 is

much different from Option 2. I do think it will be good to stick with the program for a while to try to determine what the real story is".

I said, "Now Option 5 presents a new wrinkle. The other Options will involve the police beginning the investigation after a crime is committed, hence the shooting. Option 5 includes bringing the police on board now when no crime has been committed. However, as I think about it, a crime has been committed, that of conspiracy to commit a murder. I will deal with that first.

I think that my conversations with Sgt. Carson have been nebulous enough that it probably does not constitute a crime. I am not sure at what point I would be guilty of conspiracy to commit a crime. I do not think I should ask a lawyer about that. I see that my try at humor is not successful on you Samantha". Samantha said, " this discussion is not what I would call humor. If you are trying to sweep me off of my feet, you should try another angle".

I said, "I am sorry. I know this is hard for you and I appreciate you sticking in here with me. Let me get back to Option 5. One problem I have with Option 5 is that we cannot be sure if Sgt. Carson is working alone. Another big thing is that at this point, I have no evidence and to accuse a policeman that has been with the department 35 years, would certainly have some repercussions. I do not think we have enough information to go to the police now". What do you think Samantha?"

Samantha said, "I do know a detective in the police department and have known him for several years. He seems like a good guy. However, I agree with you that we do not have much to approach him with. If we need to bring in him at some point, I can call him". I said, "Thanks Samantha, that may come in handy later. We can keep evaluating when the best time to bring him on board.

I said, that brings us to Option 6. Option 6 sounds like what we just said. We will keep going forward, while looking for the best opportunity to bring in the detective.

Samantha, now we have reviewed all the options we came up with. I would like to get your observations about the options before I summarize my thoughts.

Samantha said, "My initial thought is that I wish you could just go with Option 2 and be done with all this. I would like to get back to us developing our relationship that we were working on before this came up. I know that with the things that we talked about when discussing Option 2, there may be repercussions from Option 2. Some of them could cause serious problems. I just do not have any good ideas on how to avoid the potential problems if Sgt. Carson wants to make trouble for you".

I said, "Samantha, I agree a clean break of Option 2 would be ideal. My life up to now has been about me serving my country with nobody but my soldier buddies to worry about. When I formed my engineering company, I did have employees, but they were still not family. But when I met you, my whole world changed. And now, I really have something to lose, and I cannot bare to think about it. I cannot get the thoughts out of my mind that walking away from Sgt. Carson will have fallout in one form or another. I guess what I am thinking is that I would always have to be looking over my shoulder if Sgt. Carson goes through with the deal without me. I would be his perfect fall guy, dead or alive.

I said, "Let me sum up where I think things are. I agree with your assessment that I could not go through with the "assisted suicide" without having regrets later. It is just not me. If I do not go through with it, and Sgt. Carson and the priest call it off, I am not sure of what Sgt. Carson may be capable of. I would always wonder if the other shoe was ready to drop.

If Sgt. Carson and the priest found someone else to do the shooting, I am pretty sure that I would be the fall guy. I think he would come after me with some trumped-up charge or worse come after me with a gun. Don't get me wrong. I am a Marine and not really afraid of him, but I have to be realistic. His coming after me could include you. That I cannot allow".

Samantha said, "Does that mean that I am a Marine's girl?"

I responded that I certainly hope so.

She smiled and said "Oorah". As much as I hated to, I said back to business.

I think what I must do is to use Option 6. I will continue to meet with Sgt. Carson as if everything is progressing according to the plan. In the meantime, I will be doing things to work around his plans with a plan of my own. I will set up some things that will confuse him when it comes down to him carrying out his plan. I know he will likely plan a double cross, but I will turn it around on him.

Last of all, if it looks like he is going through with the shooting, I will make sure that I have an airtight alibi. Right before the planned incident, I will talk to your detective friend and let him know everything I know. The only problem with this plan is that he and the law may think of me as an accomplice that chickened out at the last minute. In other words, I could be considered a co-conspirator. I will try to take care of this ahead of time with the detective, but there is some risk that he may not believe that I was only going along to stop the assassination or "assisted suicide", whichever it is.

Samantha said, " I agree with what you are proposing. I think it is the only way to end this madness. I think my detective friend will work with us. He is a good guy".

I said, "Samantha that brings up another problem. If Sgt. Carson ever gets suspicious; he could follow me and that would lead to you. I cannot allow that to happen. For the time being, I am going to have to move to a hotel. We cannot be seen together in Sandton. I do not like that, in fact I hate that, but we cannot take the chance. I think we can still meet up somewhere and travel to Brandenburg a few times, but we must be very careful. If he knew about you, he could use that to force me to go through with the shooting".

Samantha started to say something, but shook her head, whispering that she understood.

I said, we will get through this. Then we will get back to our life. I do love you and will keep in regular contact. I joined her on my couch and hugged her. I said that it won't be long, and things will be different. I can still come by for a few hours during the day to work on your house. I will tell Sgt. Carson that I found a small handyman job. That way I can keep you up to date on what is going on. We kissed and hugged for a while to absorb all the feelings we could. After a while, we both said it was time to call it a night. The new plans would start tomorrow.

CHAPTER 10

SURVEILLANCE 101

I realized that I needed to know more about Sgt. Carson. The only way to learn more was to mount my own surveillance project. That will mean I will need to know where he goes, who he meets with, and it would be great to know what he talks about. That may not be possible. Following is one thing but getting close enough to hear what is being said would be much harder.

The first thing I did was to go online to EBAY to look for some magnetic mini-GPS trackers. I found several and decided on a unit that has a range of up to 10 miles and will hold its charge for up to 30 days of use and 90 days of standby. I bought 4 just in case I need more than one. I will place one of the units on Sgt. Carson's Chevy Chevelle SS so I can follow him without having to stay close-by. This unit will also alert me when there is movement on the vehicle it is installed on. This will allow me to not be so concerned about going over to Samantha's house, because I will know where Sgt. Carson is and whether he is following me.

I supposed this will put me back in my sniper routine. I will go on stakeouts to watch Sgt. Carson. It is important to understand as much as possible about who he talks to and meets with. The most important thing to learn is whether he gets a second shooter. If I can learn that, I should be able to work with Samantha's detective friend in a way that proves I am not working with Sgt. Carson.

I will have a little more freedom to go to Samantha's house with the mini-GPS trackers on Sgt. Carson's Chevy Chevelle SS. I think I will also install a security system around Samantha's house and property. I think it will be good to have a system with cameras around the outside of the house, as well as entry detection for windows and doors.

I talked to Samantha about installing the security system. She agreed that is a great idea even if there was no concern about Sgt. Carson. She grinned and said that no one would be able to sneak up on us when we are having dessert. I said I wouldn't mind some dessert now. She responded that you can only have dessert in the morning or at night.

I got back on EBAY to buy an elaborate security system. I was determined to buy the best system I could find. I would need about 10 cameras to protect the house and garage. Hopefully, it would be able to protect this property for several years. I desperately hoped I would be here to enjoy it.

While on EBAY, I decided to buy a couple more of the thumb drive recorders to record as many of my conversations with Sgt. Carson as possible. I had another thought. If I got some of those small wireless cameras that you see on TV, I could put one in Sgt. Carson's apartment. They are so small that they can hardly be seen, and it will record video and audio. There is no way to know what I may learn about Sgt. Carson. We are really in an electronic age.

I put a rush on shipment of the electronic equipment and received them the next day. Since I had been to Sgt. Carson's apartment, I knew where he lives, and I had seen his Chevelle SS. We had talked about him owning a muscle car and how many tickets he had gotten over the years. I went to his apartment complex at 4:00 am and slipped the mini magnetic GPS unit under his rear wheel well. It was not noticeable from the street.

I left and went back to my apartment. I took out my phone and turned the GPS app on. The app brought up the map of the area and there was the blinking light of the unit on Sgt. Carson's car. Now the waiting game started. I thought he would likely leave for work between 7:00 and 8:00 am, so I had some time to be studying the security system instructions. They were fairly simple but would require a considerable amount of ladder time to install all the cameras on the exterior of the house. These cameras all required electrical power, so they would need to be mounted on wood on the exterior and interior of the house. The monitor can bring up detail from each of the cameras all at once or individually selected ones. I should be able to get this system installed in the next couple of days.

As the clock approached the seven o'clock hour, I turned my attention to the GPS app. Sgt. Carson's Chevelle SS started moving at 7:15. The map showed the movement of his car along the road. The resolution was very good and since I was 6 or 7 miles from his apartment, I was very pleased with the GPS system.

I went over to Samantha's house. I told her that as a sniper I usually had a spotter. I cannot decide if you are going to be my spotter or spy. I told her about the mini-GPS on Sgt. Carson's car and that he had started moving and that the resolution was very good. I told her about the security system that I bought for her property and that I would install it in the next couple of days. She said, "I knew it would be good to have you around. And you are so cheap. Her normal grin showed up. I responded, "You have not seen my bill yet". I grinned back and I think she got my meaning.

CHAPTER 11

THE THIEVES MEET AGAIN

That night Samantha and I were getting ready for dinner when my phone alarmed. It was the GPS app. I said, Sgt. Carson is on the move. I think I will go see where he is going. Samantha said, give me 30 seconds, I will go with you. I did not see any harm in her going, so we loaded up in her RX 350 Lexus and took off. She was driving and I was watching the GPS. I still had a very good connection on my phone, and it appeared he was going toward Brandenburg. He was about ten miles ahead of us, but we began closing the gap.

When his car stopped, we were about 7 miles away. As we approached where his car had stopped, we saw it was at a Pizza Hut. Since we were in Samantha's Lexus instead of my truck, we decided to part close enough to watch the entrance to Pizza Hut.

William Jameson, Jerry Truman, and Sgt. Carson had planned to meet on Friday night. They had decided not to meet at the Lazy Goat. They met in Brandenburg, since it was only thirty miles away and they were not likely to see anyone they knew there. Sgt.

Carson noticed that William and Jerry were nervous and wanted to get down to business immediately.

Inside the Pizza Hut, Sgt. Carson began, "William, you and Jerry are both nervous. I told you I would come up with a plan and I have. My plan will take a few more days to tie up some loose ends, but when we meet with Bishop, we should tell him that we will just return the money to the church's account. We can also suggest that he see if he could set up the records to hold out enough money for him to make the move to South America. Our main objective is to settle his nerves so that he does not do something stupid".

William spoke up. "Sgt. Carson, is that your great plan? I thought we were going to avoid having to give up the church's money. I am not comfortable that Bishop can keep this to himself for long. Are you guys willing to stake your futures on his ability to not go to a confessional and spill his guts and implicate us?"

Jerry broke in, "Sgt. Carson, you said you would come up with a plan. Do you call this a plan? I have no intention of looking over my shoulder for the rest of my life, wondering when the whole house of cards comes crashing down".

After we had been there 5 minutes, Samantha said, "I am going in to see who he is meeting with". I immediately said no, but she said, "They do not know me. I will go in and order a couple of Personal Pan Supremes to go. While I am waiting, I will see if I can hear any of their conversations. Then I will come back out here. We can eat our pizza and decide who we want to follow". I could not argue with her logic, so all I could say was to be careful.

Back in the Pizza Hut, Sgt. Carson said, "Calm down fellows. I told you I have a plan. Telling Bishop that we are going to return the money is just to give me a little time to tie up the loose ends I mentioned. The bottom line is that we will not return the money. Trust me. I will bring you into the plan when I get it finalized, but we just have to convince Bishop that everything will be worked out. Some of the details of the plan will be better left unsaid. I have it under control. I will only bring you in if I need to. The less you know the better. This kind of thing falls in my line or work. That is why I am part of the group.

"Let's meet with Bishop as planned and set him at ease. The remainder of the plan will take 2 to 3 weeks to finalize. It was agreed that since I knew Bishop better than you two, it would be best if I took control of the meeting and explained the details of the plan to return the church's money. Let's plan on meeting with Bishop next Tuesday night here in Brandenburg at 8:00 pm. Have another beer and relax. See you then".

Samantha did exactly what she had said she would do. As she walked back to the car, I saw a big smile on her face. Boy, do I love her smile. When she got back in the car, she said, "I was only able to make out a portion of their conversation because they were apparently trying to be discreet. However, I will say that the conversation was somewhat heated. Oh, by the way, I was able to pretend I was talking on the phone and snap a couple of pictures of the men at the table. There were three men. One looked a little familiar, but I am not sure where I have seen him. We had a good view of the front door, so we were able to eat our pizzas and talk without worrying about missing them when they leave".

After 15 or 20 minutes, we saw the men stand up in the Pizza Hut and head for the door. I said, "Let's follow the man you think you have seen before, since we know where Sgt. Carson will likely go". We saw that all three men got into separate cars. Since I did not have a GPS unit on the man's car that looked familiar to Samantha, we would have to do our best to follow him without being seen. He was driving a late model Cadillac Escalade which should be easy to follow.

Luckily, Sgt. Carson left the parking lot first and sped off in his Chevelle SS. The man we were to follow was the last of the three to leave the parking lot, which was good.

We followed him for two or three miles. and we looked at each other and I said, "It looks like he is going toward Sandton. It is strange that at least Sgt. Carson and this guy did not ride together. I wonder why. It will be good to find out who this guy is and why they were having a heated conversation".

Samantha said, "I will try to find out who the guy is. If we can follow him to his house, we can easily find out who he is". We followed him all the way to the north side of Sandton. Samantha said, "He is going toward the country club, which is the wealthy side of town". Sure enough, he turned down Country Club Blvd. It wasn't long before he came to a gated community. We had to turn into a driveway well back to not be seen.

Samantha said "We will not be able to go any further. I will have to do my investigation online since there are many streets behind the gate".

I told Samantha not to worry, "I will come back tomorrow and see if I can get through the gate behind a resident. Once I get inside, I will ride around to see if I can spot his car. I just thought of something else. I need to rent another car. I do not want to be doing surveillance using my Ford truck or your Lexus".

Samantha spoke up, "Why don't you stake out this area tomorrow morning until the guy's Escalade comes out to go to work? You could then follow him until he parks and goes into his office. Then plant another of your GPS devices on his vehicle. That way we can see exactly where his house is and ultimately find out who he is. This will not tell us what his connection with Sgt. Carson is, but it is an important piece of the puzzle". I said, "I hope this is not a 500-piece puzzle".

I followed Samantha's advice the next morning. Sure enough, my guy came through the gate at 7:30 am, hopefully on his way to work. I followed him to downtown Sandton to the city hall. He parked on the street and went inside. Since I did not know if this is where he works, I decided to work fast to install the magnetic mini-GPS device in case he was leaving soon. When I got back to my newly rented Toyota Camry, I looked on my phone and found the app for this GPS device. It came on very strong like the first unit. I set the unit to alarm me when the subject vehicle began to move.

Having set the unit up, I was about to leave, but had a thought. I knew what he looks like, so I decided to go into the city hall to look around and see if I could spot him. He likely did not know who I am or what I looked like. Walking down the hallways it did not take long.

I saw him through the glass doorway of the City Council office. There were several people standing around talking. The body language of the people clearly indicated, he was the boss, the Chairman of the City Council. I looked at the name tag and saw that his name was William Jameson. I kept walking to not draw attention to myself, but my legs were a little weak. What had I gotten in the middle of? I cannot be sure that the meeting with Sgt. Carson had anything to do with the "assisted suicide", if that is what it is. But this was another red flag. I would have to be even more careful, for myself and Samantha.

CHAPTER 12

THE MEETING WITH FATHER BISHOP

A couple of days later, both of my GPS units alarmed at the same time. That meant that Sgt. Carson and William Jameson were both on the move. I called Samantha and told her about the alarms.

She said, "Why are we not on the move?" I had left my Camry in front of her house, so we met at the car and started up the GPS app for Sgt. Carson's car. As I expected, it seemed to be heading to Brandenburg. I switched to Jameson's vehicle, and it was also heading to Brandenburg. I thought, "Here we go again".

I said to Samantha, "One problem we have is that you have likely been seen by both of these men. We will not be able to get out of the car this time".

Samantha said, "They probably did not notice me and would not remember me". I looked at her and said, "Are you kidding me? When you walk into a room, there is not a guy in the room that will not only notice you but will remember you for a long time. We will at least see who attends this meeting".

Then I sprung my surprise on Samantha. "I get to go this

time because I have some disguise equipment. I will go into the restaurant to see who is there". We followed Sgt. Carson's car to the Steak and Ale. When we got there, we did not see Sgt. Carson's car, but he was most likely already inside. We did see Jameson park his Escalade and go inside.

I got out my disguise and showed it to Samantha. She started laughing and said, "Are you really going to use that stuff? You will look like Groucho Marx. What if they spot you"?

I said, "Only Sgt. Carson knows me, and I will make sure I avoid his line of sight". I put on the mustache and goatee beard. I put on an oversized pair of clear-lens glasses. I also had a slightly graying wig. I thought that this was enough and asked Samantha what she thought.

She said, "I think you are crazy, but as the song says, 'it may just be a crazy person I am looking for.'"

When I got into the restaurant and looked around, I saw Sgt. Carson. Luckily, his back was to me. What surprised me was that there were four men at the table. I recognized Jameson and the third man from the Pizza Hut meeting. I did not recognize the fourth man at the table. I went to the bar and ordered a drink and sat down. While sipping my drink, I was able to look around occasionally. I even took a few pictures while appearing to talk on my phone. It was a little trick I learned from Samantha. After 10 minutes, I paid for my drink and told the bartender that my party was not coming, so I would just come back another time. I left the restaurant and rejoined Samantha in the Camry.

Meanwhile, at the foursome's table, one of the men I did not know was obviously very nervous. He spoke up first, "Well, Sgt. Carson, did you figure out what we can do? So far, the guys that want to open up a school have not mentioned it again, but I don't know what to say if they do".

The other man I did not know spoke up and suggested that they all order drinks before getting down to business. Everyone ordered beers except the somewhat nervous man. He was so nervous that he ordered a double gin and tonic. After they settled in with their drinks, Sgt. Carson began unraveling his fake plan.

Carson said, "Bishop, I have looked at this from every angle I could think of. It is obvious that we cannot just do nothing. Sooner or later, someone will find out the church money is gone. Questions will start pouring in, none of which have any suitable answers. I think the only thing we can do is to replace the church money. As far as the church money, Bishop do you think anyone has any way of knowing how much money should be in the church account?"

Bishop thought for a moment and said, "No one would know the exact amount, but some of the people may have a general idea. I have handled the money for the last few years, since our treasurer retired. We have had a few wealthy members make special donations to the church. When you mentioned returning the church money, I assumed you meant all of it".

Carson responded, "Listen, Bishop, the plan I came up with is to return most of the money which I believe would be somewhere between 1.5 and 2 million dollars. Let me lay out my plan and the three of you can critique it. First, I suggest we put 1.25

million dollars back in Bishop's church account which is in the Brandenburg bank. In two or three weeks, you move the money back into the bank in Sandton.

You can explain to the two guys on the school project why you opened the account in Brandenburg, if it comes up. Do you remember we talked about how you didn't want the local bankers talking about the size of the church account? You can then tell them you agree with their proposed project, so you thought it would be better to have the money close by.

"After we have transferred 1.25 million dollars back to the church account, that will leave some of the church's money in our account. I think it is only fair that we keep some of the money for the time and trouble we have invested in our project".

Bishop started to interrupt, but Sgt. Carson held up his hand. He said, "Wait until you hear the whole plan. "Then you can make suggestions. The third part of the plan would be for you to plan a public announcement about the school project. I have even located a great property for the school and orphanage. I can show it to you next week to see what you think.

"I know you have talked about retiring to South America. Well, I think that is a good idea. Now I have to say something that is a little blunt, but I feel I must say it. I am a little nervous that if you were to stay here that you may develop a guilty conscience and confess to someone. You may go to a confessional or something like that. So, what I am proposing is that you make the public announcement about the school, get the project started, and then retire. Out of the money we hold out, you take three hundred thousand dollars and retire to South America. What do you guys think? Does it sound plausible?"

Both Jerry and William shook their heads and said they agreed that it sounded like the safest way to avoid any suspicions about what had been done over the last three years. Bishop did not appear as enthusiastic as the other three men. He said he was assuming they would return all the church funds.

Jerry spoke up, "Look Bishop, we put this plan together and have worked for three years. We can't afford to take any risks that could end up sending us to jail. It is unfortunate that the guys from the church came up with the proposed school project, but something like this was bound to happen sooner or later. It sounds like Sgt. Carson's plan will let us cut our losses and cover our tracks. It will keep the four of us in the clear and allow you to retire with a good nest egg. That much money will go a long way in South America. I say, "Let's go for it".

William turned to Bishop and said, "Bishop, we asked Sgt. Carson to come up with a plan that would keep us all above suspicion. I agree with Jerry. I think Sgt. Carson's plan is simple and will accomplish what we all need. We won't walk away with as much as we hoped for, but at least we will have something for our time and effort. And most importantly, we will be in the clear. I have to go now, but maybe you and Sgt. Carson can talk and answer any questions you may have. Keep me posted if there is anything else I need to do". Jerry said he was also going to leave, and they both got up and walked toward the door.

After Jerry and William left, Sgt. Carson could tell that Bishop was still somewhat nervous. Carson ordered a couple more drinks and tried to keep the conversation on surface things. Bishop went through his drink quickly, so Carson ordered another round. After a few minutes, Carson could tell that the drinks were beginning to take the desired effect. Bishop's taunt face began to relax. Carson asked Bishop what he would do in South America after he retired and where he would like to end up. He thought for a few seconds before answering. He then surprised Carson by saying he may open a bar or a medical clinic.

Carson said, "Those two things seemed very different. One is an entrepreneurial endeavor, and the other one is a humanitarian effort. Quite a wide range of interest".

The alcohol was beginning to work its magic on Bishop. He began talking. He said, "Opening a clinic was my first idea, you know to try to make a difference or in some way to make up for what I had done. But a side of me thought that owning a bar would give me the contact with people that I have always wanted. In some way, I hoped I might be able to help people by listening to their problems and offering good advice. Not like a psychiatrist, but like a bartender in a small, quiet bar. Does that sound crazy?"

Carson said, "No, not at all. I understand both of your ideas. The clinic would obviously help a lot of local people, wherever you were located. The main negative, off the top of my head, is that it would be pretty expensive to set up a clinic. In addition to the cost of the clinic building and equipment, you would have to hire a doctor and nurse as a minimum. If the area is poor and cannot afford to pay for medical expenses, you might run out of money sooner than expected. Since you are not a doctor, people would likely begin asking questions about what line of work you had been in. My advice to you is to avoid much discussion about your past. If they find out that you were a priest, they will naturally want to know where you served. If word got back to someone in your church, they may wonder where you got the money to start a clinic.

"Now the bar idea sounds like it would likely be self-sustaining. If you think you would enjoy that, your money could last for a long time. I do not think that your owning a bar would lead people to ask about your past. The bar could possibly even develop enough money to eventually help start and support a clinic".

I also pointed out that he was returning most of the church's money and that he was helping get a very good school project started. He had worked hard at the church for several years. I was not sure if it was my reasoning or the alcohol, but his eyes began to brighten. I asked him more about the bar idea. He confessed that he enjoyed going to bars, and talking to other people, not as a priest, but just as someone to listen to what they had to say. He felt that he often was able to give some good advice by listening to their stories and just being a good listener. He finally said, "I think you are right. The bar makes more sense to me. While the clinic would be great for the people in one of the poorer countries, I would likely run out of money within a year or two and the people would be just as bad off as before I got there".

Bishop looked up and said, "Sgt. Carson, I really appreciate your understanding and help in this matter. I feel like we can get through this now. I think I had better go before the alcohol puts me to sleep and I drive off a cliff or in a ditch on the way home".

Carson said, "Bishop, you are right, we will get through this.

Drive safely. I would hate to have to give you a ticket for driving under the influence".

We laughed and parted. Carson stayed behind and had another drink. He almost felt bad about what he had planned for Bishop. Bishop was not a bad guy, but he is weak. He cannot be trusted to protect William, Jerry, and me. We had worked hard for our retirement account and taken huge risks. It was now time to collect for our efforts. I will do what I have to do. The plan is now set in motion.

CHAPTER 13

SAMANTHA AND I HAVE A NEW PROBLEM

When I got back to the car, I looked at Samantha and said, "We have another problem. There are four men meeting in the restaurant. Three of them are the same ones from Pizza Hut. I have no idea who the fourth guy is. I did get a few pictures, but I do not know how to use them. Do you have any thoughts?"

Samantha thought for a moment then said, "It may be a long shot, but I know a lady that works at the library. She has lived in Sandton for her whole life. I will talk to her tomorrow and show her the photos we took and see if she recognizes them. We already know two. If we find out who the other two are, we can then see if we can find any reason why they would be meeting in what seems like clandestine meetings".

I said, "Since we know two of the four are from Sandton, there is probably no need to follow anyone back to Sandton". Samantha agreed, then gave me her famous grin. She said, "I think the mustache and goatee are the real you. Are you going to keep it?" We laughed and I removed the disguise paraphernalia. I did say that I may need it again and that it did give a touch of class. By the time we got back to Samantha's place, it was 10:30 so we kissed and said good night.

The next morning Samantha and I had breakfast together. She said that she did not have much scheduled, so she would go to the library. She said that she would call me if the librarian could identify the other two men. I had another meeting with Sgt. Carson scheduled later in the day, so we planned to get together for dinner.

I also thought I needed to do some handyman work. I had received the security system the day before, so I got it out and opened it up. There were a lot of parts. I hoped I was up to the task. After looking at the instructions, I realized that it was just a bunch of repeated steps. If I figured out one, then I would just repeat it 9 more times since there were 10 cameras. It took most of the day to install the 10 cameras because of having to work from ladders. I decided to hook up the monitor to the cameras the next day. I needed to prepare for the meeting with Sgt. Carson.

When Samantha returned from her day's work of talking to the librarian, she had a bewildered look on her face. I asked what the matter was, and she suggested that I sit down. She began, "The librarian knew all four men in the picture. She was curious and asked why I was asking. I told her that I knew two of them and wondered who the other two were. She seemed satisfied and said that the first was Sgt. Carson of the Sandton police department. The second was William Jameson, the Chairman of the City Council. I said that was who I thought they were. She continued that the third man was Jerry Truman, the owner of Sandton Mercedes the largest auto dealership in Sandton. I said that he had looked somewhat familiar. The fourth man was the one that floored me. He is Father Bishop, the Catholic priest in Sandton. I thanked her and left the library".

Samantha stopped to take a breath and then said, "This adds a new wrinkle to this whole plot. We knew Sgt. Carson was friends with the Catholic Priest. The new question is, why is he meeting with the other two men? Now is the time we need to develop a new set of options. The danger has elevated to a new level".

I said, "We need to think about your safety. We may need to avoid being together completely until this is over". Samantha said, " Let's not be too hasty. They still do not know about me. We do not know if the other three know about you. Remember, you have tracking GPS units on two of the guys. At this point, we do not know that these meetings are about "assisted suicide". We need to consider all our options. It may be time to talk to the detective guy I know".

I said, "You may be right. We need to talk about when to bring him in, and how much we tell him. The thing I keep thinking about is, am I already an accessory to commit murder in the law's eyes? I think when we bring your detective friend in, I need to tell him all and find out, if I am in fact guilty, now. If so, we need to reevaluate our time together. I will not allow my feelings for you to cause you to become an accessory".

Samantha looked like she wanted to object, but I raised my hand to indicate that the discussion was over. Samantha did speak up and say that she thought the best way to bring the detective into the circle was for her to call him and say that she had heard something that may involve the police department. I could ask him to come by my house to discuss it. I agreed that that was probably the best approach.

I said, "You are a very good counselor. Remind me to recommend you to my friends. Wait, I have no friends". We laughed and I gave her a kiss. I was wondering if this could be our last kiss. She sensed something was bothering me and asked what it was. I could not bring myself to tell her what my thoughts were, so I just said everything was okay.

Samantha got out her phone and dialed the police department and asked for Detective Murphy. When he came to the phone, Samantha told him she had heard something disturbing about a police officer. She wanted to know if he would mind coming by her house to discuss it. Detective Murphy remarked that it had been a while since they had seen each other, but that he would be glad to come by. Samantha said when can you come? Murphy said he could come by after lunch if she was available. Samantha said that would be great.

When Detective Murphy arrived and knocked on the door, Samantha let him in. They shook hands. I was sitting in a chair across the room. Then he saw me, and he introduced himself. Samantha said, " Sean the reason I asked you here is a little more complicated than I mentioned over the phone. Preston is doing some handyman work on my house, and he is renting my garage apartment. We have become good friends and I think it would be better for him to tell his story. Let's take a seat before he begins. Would you like some lemonade?" We all got a glass of lemonade, and I began my story.

I said, "This is a bit unusual for me, so if you have any questions, you can stop me and ask for clarifications". I told him about how I came to be in Sandton. I told him about meeting Sgt. Carson and how I had told him about my background with the Marines as a sniper and my time in the engineering business. I stopped and told him that I was now going to get to the part of my story that he may find offensive, but I hoped he would hear me out to the end. He nodded in agreement.

I told him that when I told Sgt. Carson about my having been a Marine sniper, he seemed a little too interested. He had asked a lot of questions about what it took to mentally become a sniper. We had talked for quite a while, and I did not know where it was going. I just thought he was really interested in that aspect of my Marine experience.

He then began telling me about a friend of his, a Catholic priest. He said that the priest was diagnosed with terminal cancer, and he ultimately said that the priest had only two or three months to live. This is where the story gets more serious. He asked me if I would consider helping the priest with an "assisted suicide". His request took me by complete surprise. I told him that I had not given much thought to "assisted suicide" in terminal cases because it had never involved anyone I knew.

He then went deeper into the story. He said that the priest had taken money from the church bank account to pay for treatment before he found out it was terminal with no hope for recovery. He said that the priest had thought he would be able to pay back the money after the treatments were over, but, when he got the news that it was terminal he panicked. He said that the priest had taken out a life insurance policy a year ago that would cover the money

ASSISTED SUICIDE OR MURDER?

he had taken from the church. That was when according to Sgt. Carson, he and the priest had come up with the plan for "assisted suicide". Sgt. Carson told me they discussed the priest changing his beneficiary to Carson and that Carson would then give the money back to the church after the priest's death. They thought this would salvage the priest's reputation and no one would know about his taking the money. At this point, I stopped talking to give Det. Murphy a chance to ask any questions he might have.

Sean said, "That type "assisted suicide" would not be considered legal in South Carolina. In fact, no "assisted suicide" was legal here. I think I would like to hear the rest of the story, but I think you probably should talk to a lawyer before continuing".

Samantha spoke up, "Sean, there is much of Preston's story that you need to hear, that I think will clear up some of the legal issues. We looked at the options of how to proceed".

Sean stopped Samantha and said, "Samantha, what I said about talking to a lawyer may apply to you as well as Preston. I do not want to cross some lines that may not be reversible".

I spoke up and said, "Sean, I agree. I do not want any of this to fall back on Samantha. Let me go a little further, and if you still feel we are endangering her, we will stop the discussion and you and I can continue later".

Samantha spoke up loudly and said, "Preston, while I appreciate your attempt to protect me, I will not allow you to push me aside". She turned to Sean and said, "There are things you need to hear so you can understand the predicament we are in here. I think it is time for Preston to rest and let me explain what process we went through".

Preston said, 'Sean, has she always been this 'take charge type person''. Sean answered that he did not know her that well, but she certainly seemed capable, and he was not going to stand in her way.

Samantha continued, "Although Preston had not agreed to anything with Sgt. Carson, he did start noticing several red flags popping up. One was that Preston had said he would like to talk to the priest to determine if there was a better way out of the situation. Sgt. Carson immediately said that they could not have a meeting between them. That left Preston not sure about the priest's feelings about this process, and Preston did not know if there was an insurance policy or if it would pay in this circumstance.

"This is when Preston and I sat down and made a list of options for the path forward. The list included just telling Sgt. Carson that he was not going to be involved. The first thought we came up with was that if Sgt. Carson and the priest went through with the "assisted suicide" with someone else other than Preston doing the shooting, Preston would be a perfect person to blame it on since he had his sniper experience. We decided that Preston's word against a 35-year policeman who grew up in Sandton would not carry much weight.

"The next option we talked about was to go through with the "assisted suicide", but we agreed that since he did not have a strong belief that "assisted suicide" was ethical or right, eventually it would come back to haunt him. What Preston did not tell you was why he moved to Sandton. He owned an engineering company that designed a chemical plant. Later there was an accident that resulted in an operator dying. He felt responsible and ended up selling the business, and his house and leaving the money to the operator's family. He was burdened with guilt, none of which was justified, since the ruling was that the operator died due to his not following proper operating procedures. This was the reason we both agreed that he could not have any involvement with the "assisted suicide".

"Since he could not just walk away from Sgt. Carson and the "assisted suicide", and he could not go through with it, it seemed like the only path forward was to bring you in. However, we realized we had no evidence of any wrongdoing. If we did nothing and the "assisted suicide" happened, he might still get blamed for it, but we would have nothing to bring to you. The only path forward was to play along with Sgt. Carson for a while and try to develop some real evidence of what he was planning. At this point, I will turn it back over to Preston. I just did not think he would tell you everything about his background. You guys are so macho, that you cannot admit you have feelings.

A little blushed, Preston continued, " Sean, it looked like the only safe way out was to gather more evidence of what was really going on. I got some auto GPS tracking devices to try to determine if Sgt. Carson actually went to talk to the priest. I put the GPS on his car. When I told him I had to talk to the priest to evaluate his intent to go forward with the "assisted suicide" he said he would talk to the priest. I told him that I insisted that they talk face to face.

"The next day he told me he went to the priest's office, and he would not agree to meet with me. He said he was afraid we would be seen together. Well, he did not go to the priest's office. I knew that because I knew everywhere he went that day. This is when it began to get even more complicated. That night Samantha and I followed Sgt. Carson to Brandenburg where he met with two other men. We did not know if it had anything to do with the priest, but it was an undefined piece of the puzzle.

"When the men left the Pizza Hut, I followed one of the guys that Sgt. Carson met with in Brandenburg and found out that he was William Jameson, the Chairman of the City Council. I put a GPS unit on his car the next day. A couple of days later both Sgt. Carson's and William Jameson's GPS units alarmed at the same time, meaning they both were on the move.

"Samantha and I followed them again to Brandenburg, but to a different restaurant. I will not elaborate on how, but I managed to go inside the restaurant and saw that there were four men this time. I did not know who the third guy was from the first meeting. The fourth guy was not at the first meeting, and I did not know who he was but noted that their conversation was somewhat heated or excited. I also managed to get a few photos of the four men.

"The next morning, Samantha showed the photos to a lady that had lived in Sandton for a long time. She identified all four of the men in the photos. To Samantha's surprise, the fourth man was the Sandton Catholic priest. This is when we decided we had to bring you in. One concern I have is that with other people involved, assuming they are all somehow involved, was that I may be endangering Samantha. In any event, we are in over our heads".

I concluded by saying, "Sean, I hope we have not waited too long to bring you in, but we really just wanted to gather some real evidence of wrongdoing, without going so far that we could be charged with any legal action. I was worried about becoming guilty of conspiring to commit a crime. I then became even more worried about involving Samantha for the same reasons. When I saw that the four men were meeting, I knew we were in too deep, and I was concerned about Samantha's safety. I was wondering if I should move to a hotel. I have to admit that once I got the GPS units on the two men's cars, I thought I did not have to worry about being followed to Samantha's house. Now that there are four men that may be involved in some manner, I may have to rethink moving to a hotel. That concludes my story except for answering your questions. I should also mention that I am supposed to meet with Sgt. Carson tomorrow at the shooting site. I had planned to suggest he pay some of the money he had promised so that I could lay low after the shooting. I figured that this would show definitely whether he was serious or not.

Detective Murphy said, "From what you have told me you both have not been guilty of conspiracy to commit murder. I also agree that you do not have any real evidence of a crime. And the meetings of the three or four individuals are not evidence of any crime. That being said, it is a series of odd things that do lend themselves to the conclusions you have come up with. I do know Sgt. Carson. He has been around a long time. I guess he is getting close to retirement. The fact that he has kept this conversation going this long and even visited the proposed shooting site is unnerving.

You have given me a lot to think about. I will think through this tonight and tomorrow morning. Do not meet anymore with Sgt. Carson, until I get back to you. You could still talk to a lawyer since no crime has been committed. The lawyer could give you some good advice about what not to do to avoid any complications later".

Samantha elbowed me and said, "Go ahead and ask him about helping him?" I spoke up, "Samantha and I wondered if I could go ahead with the meeting tomorrow and ask him for the up-front money. If you agreed for me to do this for you, then wouldn't I be working with you and therefore not guilty of being an accomplice?"

Sean said, "I will think about that. There may be some danger from those involved in going that far. Wait until I call you tomorrow morning before you do anything".

Preston said, "I will follow your advice to wait until you call but do not forget that I am a Marine that has been on the battlefield before. I am trained to evaluate situations and adapt when it is necessary. I really want to help end this correctly".

CHAPTER 14

PRESTON'S CHECK-UP ON DETAILS

The next day finally arrived. It had been a long night. I could not meet with Sgt. Carson until I heard from Sean. There were still so many things that did not make sense. I wished that I could check up on the insurance policy. It seemed crucial to Sgt. Carson's plan, if it were true, that the timing of the payout on the policy and returning the money to the church's bank account be handled quickly. Surely, Carson would know, if the payout on the policy got delayed for any reason, his whole thing could fall apart. The fact that the beneficiary was changed to Sgt. Carson looks like it could raise questions. And I wonder if Sgt. Carson is honest enough to put any of the insurance money into the church's account. Two million dollars is a lot of money. Questions, questions, questions. I kept reminding myself that until I was out of this process cleanly, I had to present myself as a trained sniper and therefore ask all the right questions in order not to arouse Sgt. Carson's suspicions.

As a Marine sniper, you are given an assignment and you go out and finish it. Seldom is there communication back and forth with anyone. However, as an engineer, there is a lot of back and forth to make sure things are right and there are always changes. But with this situation, there are so many unknowns that I feel like should be answered before going forward. I know this is not like the Marine sniper assignments. Here, there are no upper commanders giving assignments. It is only one man saying that another man wants an ""assisted suicide"".

Another thought kept worrying me. Sgt. Carson is a policeman. He is not rookie cop, but a sergeant. It seems like he approached me about this "assisted suicide" awfully soon after meeting me. For all he knew, I could run to the authorities with his plan. I know he would be able to dismiss my allegations as some crazy new guy, but it would put a stop to his whole plan. It was just another one of those strange feelings I had about his plan. Part of me wished I had run away from this as fast as I could, but I didn't have any place to run to. Now with Samantha in the picture, I had too much to lose to make any mistakes that could jeopardize what we already had together and hoped we would have together later.

As the hours passed, I continued to think instead of sleeping. Who knows what type of story Sgt. Carson could dream up? He could say I had approached him about a plan to assassinate Father Bishop. Well, enough of that. I am to meet Sgt. Carson at the proposed sniper's nest in a few hours. That will give me time to walk to the street to check out things like the sun location, prevailing winds, glares and potential escape routes, so that I can carry on my charade with Carson. I know Sgt. Carson says he has things worked out, but worked out for whom? My training as a sniper taught me to have an escape plan and a backup in case things did not progress as planned. In the military, assignments often do not follow the plans precisely, hence the saying "overcome and adapt".

The night ended for me at 5:00 am. As I walked down the street in front of Cary's store and the proposed school building, I had to admit it was not a bad location. It was a relatively short shot with a good line of sight. I did not detect any wind tunnel effects and glare would not be a factor in late afternoon. Sgt. Carson had done a good job of choosing this site. From the ground this site looked like it would work. If Sean Murphy calls and says it is okay to meet with Sgt. Carson, I will take the next step and meet with Sgt. Carson at the shooting site above the store to add one more piece to the puzzle.

About 10:00 am, Sean Murphy called me. He said that while it could include some danger, it would probably be best to meet with Sgt. Carson today and not let on that I was having second thoughts. You and Samantha were right that if he passed money to me, he was definitely guilty of conspiracy to commit murder. Since I was working with Sean, that would effectively make me an informant doing undercover work. He asked me if I wanted to wear a wire to the meeting. I said that I would rather not wear a wire because it might make me nervous and give away what I was trying to do. I said that I would get back in touch with him after my meeting today. He said we should meet at Samantha's house at 7:00 tonight. His final words were, be careful.

Sgt. Carson was right on time at 3:00 pm. We met at the back of the store at the stairway to the second-floor vacant space. I was not sure where or how he got a key to the second-floor space.

That was a loose end I would have to get answered. As we walked up the stairs, I noticed the stairs were behind some shrubs that gave some reasonable cover. When we got to the top of the stairs my question about the key was answered. No key was necessary, because the lock was not operable. I asked Sgt. Carson about a possible vagrant in the space today or on the event day. He said that they had cleared vagrants out 6 months ago and had not had any since. He also said that he would check it out on the day of the event when he brought the sniper's rifle to the space.

I stopped Sgt. Carson and said, "that will not work for me. I need to get the rifle two or three days before the event. I have a lot of things I need to check out with the rifle". Sgt. Carson thought about it and then said he understood. He said he would arrange a place to meet so he could give me the rifle.

As we walked around the space, Sgt. Carson mentioned that the space between the store's ceiling and the floor on this level was well insulated and was deep enough for the air condition and heating ducts. We could not hear any noises from the store below. I told Carson that was one concern I had before I got to the space. I said, "After the shooting, if I had to hurry across the wood floor, I would not want to be heard from below". Of course, I would not be doing the shooting, but to keep things moving forward until Samantha, Sean and I figured out what to do, I had to assume the position of a sniper. That meant planning out every detail. If I showed any hesitation Sgt. Carson could alter his plans and I would not know what to do.

Next, we looked at the location for the sniper's nest on the north side of the building. It had a perfect line of sight to the proposed area for the announcement for the school, which was diagonally across the street. The windows were already covered so that would give good concealment. As we walked out, I noticed windows on the west side of the building overlooking the street below. Sgt. Carson noticed that I looked at the windows on the western wall. He said he would have a car waiting at the back corner of the store on the side street. The car would be a navy-blue Honda Accord. After the shooting, he said that I should leave the rifle in the sniper's nest and cross over to the stairway. I could get in the car and drive to Summerville. He said that he would arrange for a realtor to show me a house that was for rent. I was to tell the realtor I was planning to move there. This would establish and alibi for me, even though he was going to personally steer the search for the shooter in the opposite direction.

Sgt. Carson asked if I had any questions. I responded, "No, this all seems pretty clear cut. But there is one thing. We talked about the $ 100,000 fee. I need half up front and half after completing the assignment". He looked taken back and said that he thought we could take care of that after.

I looked him in the eyes and said, I don't think you are that naive. The fee is not negotiable, unless you are wanting to pay more than the $ 100,000, which I will consider. Sgt. Carson started to say something but was perplexed. I laughed and said I am joking. His relief was immediate.

He said that he had an associate that had access to money that he was going to loan me for a few months. Sgt. Carson told his friend it was for a construction project he was doing but had to keep it confidential. Sgt. Carson said his friend will have the initial payment of $ 50,000 in one-hundred-dollar bills and will meet you at the Sandton Steak House on Magnolia Street at 4:00 pm on Thursday, two days from now. That will give him enough time to get the money together. He will be wearing an Atlanta baseball cap. You can be sitting at a table alone. He will sit down and will give you the money in a small paper shopping bag from Cary's department store. No conversation will be necessary. He will be instructed to leave before you. After a few minutes, you can leave the restaurant. If there are any problems, you can give me a call.

Sgt. Carson asked, do you have any questions, Preston? I said no, let's get out of here. I would not want anyone to think I am here to lease this space. As we walked toward the door to the stairway, I saw another door off to the west side of the room. I didn't let on that I had noticed it, but I figured I could check it out later. I was surprised that he didn't mention it, but I guessed he was not a detailed person and was in a hurry to get out of the building.

CHAPTER 15

A FEELING OF UNEASINESS

I am not sure if it was my military training or my work as an engineer that made me not like loose ends, but there were quite a lot of loose ends in this whole plan. After meeting with Sgt. Carson at the sniper's nest, warning bells and whistles were going off. I knew I should just walk away and tell Sgt. Carson I wanted no part of this. However, as Samantha, Sean and I had discussed, we would never be sure that Sgt. Carson would try to pin the blame on me.

As we had already concluded, if I told Sgt. Carson I wanted no part of this, he could just find someone else to do the job and figure out a way to put the blame on me. That brought me back to Samantha and my conversation about the options. What Sgt. Carson did not know was that I had a recording thumb drive of us discussing the ""assisted suicide"". I could tell him I had the recording. That could go one of two ways. The first and least likely way would be to call off the whole plan. He obviously could not arrest me for a plan to commit murder because that would implicate himself. The second and most likely way Sgt. Carson could react would be to find someone else to complete the job and then kill me or have me killed to pin the blame on me. Samantha and I had come to that conclusion several days ago and it still seemed logical. It seemed that Detective Murphy also agreed, but I was not completely sure he believed everything I had told him.

I had a feeling the second way out for Sgt. Carson would be the chosen method. The fact that he was with the police department means that he would have access to ways and tools that could be used against me. Also, he might have access to some unscrupulous type guys that could possibly take care of the "assisted suicide" and maybe me as a side job. All in all, it seems I have gotten myself into a mess. Sgt. Carson knows I was a sniper, and I am not from the area. My only salvation could be the recording of our conspiracy conversation. The thing about me telling him about the recording could possibly backfire on me. He might be able to convince the powers at be that he was investigating some rumors he had heard or something I had said while drinking at the local bar. With the recording I made of the discussion I had with Sgt. Carson, I could bring him down with me, but that would mean that I went down also. I think I need to keep the thumb drive recorder as my secret trump card up my sleeve.

The fact that I had only known Sgt. Carson for a couple of months, and he asked me to shoot a Catholic priest is at best unnerving. To top that off, he is a policeman. I am not allowed to talk to the man I am supposed to assist in his suicide. I cannot check up on his medical condition or his life insurance. If all Sgt. Carson said about Father Bishop was true, I could understand his predicament. I could even sympathize about how he convinced himself that taking the church's money was only temporary. While I know it didn't make it right, I still felt sorry for him and the situation and especially considering the cancer.

It almost seemed like a 'B' grade movie with washed up actors. I didn't like to think of myself as a washed-up individual, but I had walked into this 'B' grade movie and got pulled in too deep before I realized it.

I once again was thankful for having met Samantha and the developing relationship. Her help in talking through how to work my way out of this mess was the only thing that kept me from going over the edge.

I cannot get the possibility of me being set-up to take the fall for murder out of my head. Sgt. Carson is a policeman. He was quick to tell me he could direct the investigation in another direction, looking for someone else. He could just as easily direct the manhunt towards me. After all, he knew my life story and about my training as a sniper. Even I could make a solid case against me that would fit my background.

In many ways, I felt more settled in the war zone in Afghanistan with enemies all around me than I did now. Here, I have no idea who my enemies are. Although Samantha and I are making progress, there are still too many unknowns.

I feel stupid for not just walking away from the beginning. At this point, I think a pretty good case could be made against me for conspiracy to commit murder. In fact, my recording of our conversation makes this an open and shut case against Sgt. Carson and me. Maybe I should destroy the tape and just tell Sgt. Carson that I have it. That way I can keep Sgt. Carson from doing something stupid while getting rid of the actual evidence. However, he might just shoot me and hope that the tape never shows up. I probably should talk to Sean about this. Maybe a better thought would to be to talk to a lawyer as Sean had suggested.

CHAPTER 16

A PLAN WITHIN A PLAN

After Sgt. Carson and I had met at the proposed shooting site and gone our separate ways, I went to our favorite bar and had a beer. It was 5:00 o'clock, which is a respectable time for drinking beer. It was a couple of hours before Samantha, Sean and I were to meet for dinner. As I was drinking my beer, I thought back to what Sgt. Carson said about meeting his associate to transfer the first $ 50,000 payment to me. Meeting in the middle of the day in a public place seemed strange. That added another question to my ever-growing list of strange things. I decided it was time for me to increase my insurance against possible setups that could put me in hot water. I had nothing concrete against Sgt. Carson's plan but decided to setup my own plan of defense.

The first thing I wanted to develop was a plan for the money transfer. I had some experience with some of the local online classified sites. I decided I could run an advertisement on Marketplace or a similar site selling some software using my local email address. I could then go to the public library and send myself an email agreeing to buy the software and agree on a price of $

300 in cash. I would have $ 300 in one-dollar bills in my pocket when I met Sgt. Carson's associate.

My bank is on the same street as the steak house just three blocks away. Before I leave the steak house, I will go to the restroom and take the $ 50,000 from the bag, put the large bills in my jacket pockets and put the three hundred one-dollar bills in the paper bag. I can then walk down to the bank and deposit the $ 300 in my personal checking account. I can't explain why I thought that Sgt. Carson might be filming the money transfer, but I guess it is what I would do if I were he. I decided to go off script and follow my own little plan and would tell the guy with the money that the software we discussed is on the thumb drive that I slide to him. This is just for someone that may be recording the incident. He will have no idea of why I am giving him a thumb drive, but he will not want to refuse it to draw attention to us.

The next step after depositing the $ 300 in the bank is to figure out what to do with the $ 50,000. Since Sgt. Carson does not know about my apartment at Samantha's place, I will buy a small safe and keep it there. If it happened to be a setup, I am sure Sgt. Carson would want to get the money back. This made it even more important that he not know where I am living. I did not want to think that he was setting me up, but I needed to take as many precautions as possible.

I met Samantha and Sean at 7:00 pm at her place to eat dinner as we had planned. We had a pleasant dinner and then Samantha reiterated what she had learned at the library. She had gone to the library to meet with the librarian and show her the pictures. She recognized all four of them. We of course knew Sgt. Carson and William Jamison, the Chairman of the City Council. The third man was Jerry Truman, the owner of the Mercedes auto dealership. She said that the fourth man was in fact Father Bishop, the Catholic priest in Sandton. Samantha broke the silence and said, "This adds another complexity to this whole situation. I think we need to go back and review our options".

I agreed but said that I needed to tell you and Sean about my meeting with Sgt. Carson at the shooting site. After I relayed the meeting with Sgt. Carson and answered their questions, I told them that I wanted to go back by the bar to see if Sgt. Carson was there. If he is there, I will tell him that I need to talk to Father Bishop prior to the event. Sgt. Carson will say that he does not think it is a good idea for me to meet with Father Bishop. I will tell him that I understand, but I insist that he talk to Father Bishop face to face tomorrow. I want to make certain that the priest is sure this is what he wants to do. I will tell him that I expect to hear from him tomorrow night whether he will meet with me. I am sure that Sgt. Carson will agree to go see Father Bishop tomorrow.

Sean said that he did not see any problem with this meeting and would be anxious to hear what happens tomorrow. I said, there is one thing left that I need to share with you, Sean. When I was talking with Sgt. Carson, we discussed the subject of the priest giving me some money to allow me to go away for a few weeks after the "assisted suicide" to basically, lay low while the investigation cools down. We agreed on an amount. That money transfer will transpire in a few days. Do you think this will automatically make me an accomplice? Does the fact I am kind of working with you make a difference?"

He thought about that for what seemed like an eternity. He finally said, "I think I should talk to a lawyer, not using or details, but get a legal opinion. I will call you tomorrow afternoon".

He left, and Samantha and I decided to have a glass of wine before I went back to my apartment. When I looked at Samantha, I could tell that she was worried. I told her not to worry. Things were falling into place and working with Sean had been a really good idea. He will guide us through this. He will be our witness that we have nothing to do with this. In fact, we are working with him. We decided it was time to get some rest, so we kissed and said good night. While walking to the garage apartment, I realized that based on the shallow kiss, we both were somewhat worried and not our normal selves. Maybe a night's rest will help alleviate some of the concerns we both have.

I did make a quick run to the bar to see if Sgt. Carson would be there. Sure enough, he was there. I got beer and sat down with him. I told him that I had been thinking that I did need to meet with the priest to evaluate his state of mind. Carson repeated that the priest did not want to meet because they could be seen together and that would ruin the whole plan. I said that I insisted that he talk to the priest again face to face to stress how important it was to me. He said he would tomorrow but did not hold out any hope.

The next morning, I was in place by 4:30 am to see if Sgt. Carson would visit Father Bishop. With my GPS unit turned on I was ready to see what would happen. At 7:30 am he left his apartment dressed in his police uniform. He drove and I followed, but he went to the police station. My hope for a short stake-out was not going to happen. He did not leave the police station until lunch time. He left but went to a fast-food establishment and returned to the station to eat his lunch. I was familiar with this type of stakeout, so I had my food and snacks. While he was eating his lunch, I made a pit stop at a nearby service station and then returned to my lookout post. Patience is a job requirement on assignment, so I didn't mind. As it turned out, my patience was required. After lunch Sgt. Carson returned to the police station. Sgt. Carson did not leave the station until 5:15 pm.

While following him to his apartment, he called me to say he had met with Father Bishop at the church office. Father Bishop had reiterated that he did not want to meet with me to avoid any potential problems with his life insurance payment. I said "OKAY". He seemed satisfied. That told me what I needed to know. Since Carson obviously had not gone to Father Bishop's office but told me he had, there was more going on that he was not willing to share with me. It seems that he is planning to complete his plan. My problem is that I do not know what his real plan is.

While thinking through the various scenarios that could take place, one thing that was fairly clear. Sgt. Carson plans on going through with the ""assisted suicide"". The thing that was not clear was whether Sgt. Carson was planning on my being the assassin or if he had a backup with me as the fall guy. One idea began to crystallize in my mind. I needed to establish an air-tight alibi for the time of the event, if it really happens.

I called Samantha and told her about my insisting that Sgt. Carson talk to the priest about meeting with him in person in the bar last night. As Samantha and I had discussed, we knew he would likely not talk to him, but we wanted to see what his response was. I told her about him outright lying to me about going to the priest's office to discuss my meeting him.

Samantha spoke up, " Preston, you need to be very careful. He has something going on and we do not know what it is. I am afraid that if he gets suspicious that you are on to him, he may decide to take you out of the picture". I told her that I understood her concern and that I would be extra careful. I told her that I would call Sean and let him know about Sgt. Carson lying about talking to Father Bishop. I also told her that I was going to cook dinner tonight and that I should be back in about an hour.

When I got back to the apartment at Samantha's place, I started the charcoals. I was trying to lay out a path forward in my mind so I could sound convincing and confident to Samantha. Nothing real concrete came to mind. We just had a good steak and wine and a lot of enjoyable conversation. There was a little dessert that followed. She is quite a lady, which is all I will say.

CHAPTER 17

MY SECOND VISIT TO THE SNIPER'S NEST

The next day I decided to check out the extra door that I had spotted when in the second-floor area. I am not sure why I wanted to check the area out, since I had decided not to go with Sgt. Carson's plan. I guess it is so I can know all the details of the area.

I drove my rent car and parked it several blocks down the street and in the parking garage. I hoped since it was a Toyota Camry it should not attract attention. I carefully walked around to the back of the Cary building and not seeing anyone I went up the stairs to the second floor. I hoped that there was not anyone up there and my wish was granted. I went in and turned the doorknob of the extra door. Surprisingly, it turned and opened up into a small area with a set of stairs going down to the first floor. My curiosity got the best of me, so I went down the stairs. There was another door that I assumed went into Cary's store. I gently turned the knob to see if it would open. The knob turned, but there was evidently a deadbolt on the door, locked inside Cary's store. I would have to investigate the door from the other side and hope that it was a single cylinder type and not a keyed lock. I went back up to the second floor and carefully opened the door to make sure no one had seen followed me up there. Again, fortune was on my side, and no one was there. I would need to tell Sean about this room so that he could investigate in case there was a shooting, and this was a potential hiding place.

I went back down the back stairs and walked around to the front of the store. My heart was beating a little fast at this point, so I decided to meander around the store to let my heart get back to normal. It was an old timey general store with all kinds of interesting things. It had men's and women's clothes, shoes, knives, children's toys and all kinds of camping equipment. It reminded me of a Mass General Store I have been in many times before.

Another part of my plan within a plan began to develop in my mind. If the lock on the door in Cary's store was really a bolt action and it could be left unlocked, it would give someone a second escape route. Always a good thing for Sean to be on the alert for. So, I made my way back to that southwest corner of the store and spotted the door. Sometimes when everything seems to be going your way is when you should get extra cautious. The lock was a bolt action type. I will have to come by on the event day and unlock it. I then realized that I was thinking like someone that was going through with the "assisted suicide". It was like I was in a daze. I am not back in Afghanistan. I am not a sniper anymore. I need to stay away from This place. I will leave it locked so it cannot be used as an escape route.

Back at my apartment, I began trying to think through the remainder of my plan. I need to get the ad in the classified website now and go to the library tomorrow to send myself the response

ASSISTED SUICIDE OR MURDER?

to the ad. Also, I need to figure out what to do with the $ 50,000. I thought about opening a bank account in Brandenburg after I get the first payment. However, depositing $ 50,000 in cash would be a red flag and raise a lot of questions, plus be reported to the United States government due to money laundering and terrorist alerts. That would be the last thing I needed was for the FBI to come knocking on my door to ask if I was a terrorist.

Since I had not detected anyone following me to Samantha's garage apartment, I did not think that Sgt. Carson knew about my apartment. I will go ahead with my original plan to buy a small room safe and keep the $ 50,000 in it. I will buy the safe after I am finished with the bank and the $ 300 deposit.

Later in the afternoon, Sean called to let me know what the lawyer had said. After going back and forth, the lawyer finally said that while it was an unusual, that if the money were turned over to Sean immediately, he said that would set the plan in motion for him working with me as an informant. Sean and I agreed that I could turn the money over to him and he could give me a receipt, showing the date and time and amount of the money.

I was somewhat relieved that I would not have to hide the money and also that it would make it clear that we were working together. It did seem like things were coming together.

CHAPTER 18

THE MONEY TRANSFER

After two days to think about the money transfer the day finally arrived. After today, I will officially be an accomplice to the "assisted suicide", or just call it what it is, murder. On the other hand, I am sort of working with Detective Murphy. Up to now, I could just say that I did not take Sgt. Carson seriously. However, when money changes hands, there is no turning back.

When I say, "No turning back," I am discounting that there is always the field decision to terminate the mission if things change in the target zone. I realized that I was thinking as if I were actually going to go through with this. I still have to figure out when to inform Sgt. Carson that I am not going through with the shooting. I also realized that if I had not met Samantha, I may very well be planning to go through with it.

Since this is money transfer day, I decided to arrive at the steak house early to scope the area and to see if I can spot anyone with a camera. However, now days anyone with a phone has a camera. It seems that nothing is private. As I walked in, I asked the host if

I could have the booth at the back of the restaurant. From there I could see everyone entering the restaurant.

Since I was early and did not want to look suspicious, I order a beer. It was 2:45 pm so the restaurant was fairly empty. I felt my pocket and noted that I had the empty thumb drive I was planning to give the bag man. Based on where I was sitting, I knew that anyone wanting to take pictures of the money exchange would have to be towards the front of the restaurant. I still did not see anyone that was interested in me. Maybe I was just being paranoid.

At the appointed 3:00 pm a man with a red baseball cap and a brown bag walked in. He looked around and spotted me. As he walked toward me, I noticed that he was very non-chalant. He was either very good at what he was doing or had no idea that he had $50,000 in the paper bag.

He sat down and said, "You Preston?" I nodded my head, and he passed the bag over to me. I could tell he was about to get up to leave, so I passed the thumb drive over to him and I said at a reasonable volume, "The software is on the drive. If you have any questions, just give me a call". He looked perplexed but said nothing. He picked up the thumb drive and slid it in his pocket and left. Like I figured earlier, he did not want to cause anyone to notice us. I remained at my table and finished my beer as casually as I could manage. I then got up and went to the rest room to swap the $ 50,000 to my jacket pocket and put the 300 one-dollar bills in the paper bag. I inspected my jacket to make sure that there were no suspicious bulges and left to go to the bank.

The bank was only two blocks away, but it seemed like two

miles. I could not help feeling nervous carrying so much money around in my pockets. I went over my speech for the bank teller in my head all the way to the bank. When I got inside the bank, I spotted a teller that I had met when I moved to town and set up my bank account.

I approached her, "Hello, Cindy how are you today?" She responded, very well. How can I help you. I haven't seen you since we set up your account. I said that I had not had much banking business yet. I guess I need to get a job. "I have to make a deposit, and I am a little embarrassed. I sold some software and ended up with three hundred dollars in one-dollar bills". Cindy laughed and said, "That is not a problem. I have a machine that does the counting for me".

I tried to look relieved and told her that I had not had a chance to count it to make certain it was all there. The machine counted the money and confirmed that it was $ 300. Cindy asked if I wanted to deposit it all and I said that I did. She made the deposit and gave me the receipt. I thanked her and left.

I called Sean and told him that I had the money and would like to meet with him to get it off my hands. He said he would come by Samantha's place around 7:00 pm. He would give me a receipt to show that he was taking possession of the money as evidence of the intent to comment murder.

When Sean arrived, we all agreed it was Miller time. It had been an eventful day and we were all a little high strung. After we took a few sips of our beers, I said, "Well the money transfer went very well. There weren't any hic-ups. I got up and went to the kitchen counter and got the $ 50,000. We counted it carefully, twice before putting it in a bag. Sean handed me the receipt that the lawyer had suggested to be part of the transaction. Sean explained to Samantha why the lawyer had suggested the receipt, and that the money would be put in the evidence room for safe and secure keeping. He mentioned that the lawyer said that this way it would be clear that I was working with Sean. Samantha gave a big sigh of relief. She said, "I have been worrying about this since the beginning. I was afraid what a crooked police office might be able to do to blame the whole mess on Preston.

I spoke up and said, "Sean, there is one thing that I need to do. I need to meet with Sgt. Carson to get the sniper rifle to complete the ruse of me being the shooter". Sean said, "As best as you can, try to not touch the rifle where Sgt. Carson handles it. It would be good to have his fingerprints on the rifle, minus yours of course".

I said, "I will do that. I hate to be a party pooper, but it is getting late. It has been a long day. I suggest we call it a day. I think I had better do some handyman work on the house tomorrow or I might get fired. I do not feel like I am earning my keep. I will start replacing the soffits that are rotting. I need something to take my mind off all that is going on with us for a few hours".

We all said good night and Sean left. Samantha and I decided to have one more beer. The tension between us had subsided. Knowing that we were officially now legally working with Sean removed the subconscious fear that we may be held partially responsible for the murder of the priest. We said our good nights and I went back to my apartment.

CHAPTER 19

LAST MINUTE PREPARATIONS

The next morning Samantha and I ate breakfast together. She asked, "Are you really going to work on the house today?"

I said, "I think I do need to do something to take my mind off this mess. It may surprise you, how driving nails into wood boards relieves stress better than drinking. I imagine that it would not be the same if I made my living that way, but it is a great part-time business.

When I started working on the house, Samantha wouldn't leave my side. She always seemed to be able to talk about things that would not be considered small talk. She was really an amazing person. The funny thing is that she was able to keep me talking without it appearing like she was drawing the words out of me. The day seemed to pass very fast. Before we realized it, it was time to eat dinner. I told her that I needed to go to the bar to see if I could connect to Sgt. Carson about getting the rifle.

She nodded and said she understood. She added, "Hurry back. The dessert bar closes".

I said, "You, really know how to put pressure on me". I got up and left.

I went back to the bar hoping to see Sgt. Carson. Sure enough, he was there. I got a beer at the bar and walked over to his booth. I noted that there were not many people in the bar and none in the area around his booth. I asked if I could join him, and he said have a seat.

He asked if we needed to go somewhere more private, but I said that it was private enough here. I told him that it had been a long day and I would likely turn in early. Since there wasn't anyone near our booth, I said that I had met with our mutual friend and that the meeting went well and that the only thing left was for me to get the special package. Sgt. Carson carefully looked around and said, " I will leave it in the Honda at the appointed place". I said, "No, I need it a couple of days early. Just normal procedures".

Carson said, "We can meet at the State Park in the camping area tomorrow around noon. No one will be around since it is too early for campers to be there". We agreed, and I stood up and said, "I am going to turn in for the night".

What I did not tell him was that I was going to my car and check the GPS app to make sure he was not going to follow me. He did not follow me, but he did leave the bar soon after I did. I decided to follow him to see if he was going to his apartment. He actually was going in the opposite direction.

I was glad I had decided to follow him. I don't know what I expected him to do, but he drove about 5 miles. He came to an abandoned parking lot for an old bowling alley.

He pulled alongside of another car and rolled down his window.

I had to pull over down the street behind a bunch of bushes. I got out of my car and tried to see who he was meeting, but I was too far away to get a look at who was in the other car. I could make out the tag number, so I wrote it down. They talked for about 15 minutes. Sgt. Carson left the parking lot first. I decided to follow the other person to see if I could gather any more information.

I had to stay back far enough to make sure he would not suspect I was following him. After about 5 more miles, he pulled into a trailer park. I had to keep going to avoid arousing suspicion. I had his tag number and where he lives, so maybe Sean could find out who he is.

I immediately called Sean and told him of my meeting with Sgt. Carson. I recounted most of my discussion with Sgt. Carson. I also told him about following Sgt. Carson after leaving the bar and how he had met with a man, that I did not know. I did give Sean the man's car tag number and told him that he went to the Magnolia Trailer Park. I asked, "Do you think you can find out from the tag number, who he is? It would be good to know if he is a local and anything you can find out about him". He said that he would run the information through the system to see what turned up, and he reminded me to be very careful. He emphasized it would be dangerous for Sgt. Carson and whoever this guy is to know that I was on to them.

I said that I would be careful, and I reminded him that my sniper training taught me how to "see, but not be seen".

The one other thing I decided to tell him was that I was to meet Sgt. Carson at the State Park campground tomorrow at noon to get the sniper rifle that Sgt. Carson was furnishing. I told him I would like to meet with him tomorrow afternoon at my apartment at Samantha's place to discuss a couple of things. We agreed to meet at 2:00 pm.

After we got off the phone, I went back to my apartment at Samantha's place. Her lights were still on, so I knew that she was still up. I knocked on her door. She opened the door and smiled her big smile. What a beautiful sight at the end of the day. I told her that seeing her smile was the best way to end the day, except maybe for a glass of wine with her.

Her smile, changed to her grin. She said, "I haven't had enough dessert lately. You are falling down on your job". I said, "I do not consider having dessert with you as part of my job, but I do work for you. I will promise to get you caught up on dessert". When we kissed, I realized that I was also behind on my dessert. I said, "I think it is going to take a long time to get caught up". She responded," I have no place I would rather be than here with you".

The next morning, I explained to Samantha what my plans for the day were. I told her that I was to pick up the sniper's rifle and then meet back here with Sean at 2:00 pm. She said she was available to meet with us, but she wanted me to be careful. It seems like everyone is always telling me to be careful. They just do not know me very well. Careful is my middle name.

At 11:30, I got settled in my truck to go pick up the rifle. I checked the GPS and Sgt. Carson was on the move. We were only 15 minutes from the State Park. I called Sgt. Carson and told him I was on the way. We agreed that he would wait at the entrance for me. We arrived within a couple of minutes of each other, and I followed him in. When we got to the camping area, it was vacant. We got out and I met him at the trunk of his car. He got the rifle out and a box on ammunition. I looked at the rifle and told him it looked like a good middle-of-the-road sniper rifle. We confirmed that all was a go and agreed on Friday at 3:00 pm, two days from now.

I confirmed that he was to leave the Honda at the side of the store on late Thursday night. He gave me the business card of the real estate agent in Summerville that he had arranged to meet with me at 3:45 pm to show me some rental houses, to establish my alibi. I told him to let me know if anything changed with the priest. He reiterated that he and the priest had setup the public announcement about the church building the boarding school across the street from Cory's mercantile store.

I told him that I would leave the rifle in the sniper's nest because I did not want to be seen leaving the building with a rifle right after the shooting. He said that would be good and help establish the fact that he could say he had seen the sniper fleeing rapidly after the shooting. After agreeing that everything seemed to be in place, I put the rifle in my truck. I turned to Sgt. Carson and said, "what will we do about the remainder of the fee". He said that he would call me to set up a convenient time and that he would be able to update me about the investigation. He said that it would probably be best to wait for three or four days to meet for the final payment, just to be sure that everything had settled down.

CHAPTER 20

PREPARING FOR THE STRIKE

Thursday night, the day before the "assisted suicide" I planned to go to the site and specifically to the sniper's nest. I wanted to do two things. First, to see if Sgt. Carson left the Honda escape vehicle where it was supposed to be, and second to drop off the sniper's rifle at the sniper's nest.

Sean, Samantha and I were to meet at 2:00 pm at Samantha's house to confirm what I was going to do with the sniper's rifle and what I should do to set up my alibi. After meeting with Sgt. Carson and picking up the rifle, I went back to my garage apartment. Samantha and I got together at her place. I showed her the sniper's rifle because she had never seen one. She was not afraid of guns and had shot many types of guns with her father. When I told her the range that snipers often had to shoot, she was amazed. I showed her how to adjust for windage and compensate for other factors like elevation differences. She said she would like to shoot a rifle like this one in the future.

When Sean arrived, we settled into Samantha's living room to discuss all that we had to do. I started the discussion with the fact that I had picked up the rifle from Sgt. Carson and that he had said that everything was a go as far as Father Bishop, was concerned. He said he would leave the Honda at the agreed upon site tonight. I reiterated that I did not know for sure if he was planning on me doing the shooting or if he had contracted someone else. I mentioned again that he had met with a guy in the abandoned bowling alley parking lot but had no way to know if it had anything to do with the scheduled ""assisted suicide"".

I then said, "Sean, I had told Sgt. Carson that I would leave the sniper's rifle in the sniper's nest. I intend to take it there tonight. Before I do, I am going to take out the firing pin. I do not think he will notice that it has no firing pin. Therefore, this rifle will not be used by anyone to be part of the ""assisted suicide"". I intend to wipe all my fingerprints off the gun where I have touched it. Some of his prints may still be on it. I did notice that the rifle has been fired recently, but not by me. This means that whoever fired the rifle may have left fingerprints on the trigger or other places".

Sean said, "I have an idea for you to consider. What about me leaving some of my fingerprints on the rifle, just not on the trigger. If Sgt. Carson suggests lifting the prints on the gun, he will not know they are mine. Hopefully, he will think he has your prints that can be used to prove that you were the shooter".

I smiled and said, "I like it. It will give him a rabbit trail to go down that will give him more time and chances to make a mistake. At this point, if there is not another shooter, he will just collect the rifle and keep it for future use. If there is another shooter, he will plan to use the rifle to build the case against me".

Sean said, "Be sure not to give him an opportunity to capture your fingerprints, if you have not already left your fingerprints on anything".

I said, "I have been to his apartment and had a few beers, so if he thought of it, he could already have mine".

I looked at Samantha and said, "You are very quiet. Do you have any comments or questions?" She said, "No, I find this interesting and scary at the same time. I do not like the fact that he may have planned all along to get your fingerprints and can now begin to build a case against you. Isn't there any way to put an end to this madness? I am afraid for you, and I am also afraid for us. Do you understand what I am saying?"

I looked her in the eyes and said, "I certainly understand, and I have some of the same feelings. However, I do not see a good way out, without going through with what has been set in motion. Let's not forget. At this point, there are several possibilities. One is that there will be no ""assisted suicide". I I cannot for the life of me understand why Sgt. Carson would have gone this far if he did not plan to go through with it. Why would he try to set me up for something that did not happen? He didn't know me when we first met in the bar. He could not have had anything against me.

"Then there are the questions about why were he and the other three men meeting, especially Father Bishop? The confusing thing is if he thinks I am going through with it, why would he be meeting with Father Bishop and the other two men? If this is the case and I do not go through with it, what happens next?

"The next possibility is that Sgt. Carson did hire someone else to do the shooting or has another person as a backup if I do not go through with it. Either way he could still plan to pin it on me. Sean, does that about sum up the situation?"

Sean thought for a moment and said, "From the information we have in front of us, I think we have to assume the "assisted suicide" will likely take place. We cannot be sure of how or exactly when and certainly we do not know who would actually do the shooting. One thing is for sure. You need to be out of the area and establish a rock-solid alibi. The thing I am not sure about is what I need to do to stop the shooting. I do not have any solid evidence of who are all the parties involved, because of the meetings that have taken place. I do agree that you should put the rifle in the sniper's nest without the firing pin and with all your fingerprints removed. How do you plan to establish your alibi?"

I said, "I think I will go to Myrtle Beach tomorrow morning early and register in a beach front motel. I might even would take a friend with me, if I had a friend". Samantha saw my grin and said, "Since you have no friends, I could possibly go with you, just so there would be a witness that you were there". She looked at me and grinned as she hit me on the shoulder. Sean said that he thought that would be a good idea, you know to establish a witness and all.

I turned to Sean and asked, "Could you keep us posted if anything happens? When do you think we should come back to town? Another thing, do you think this could in any way backfire on Samantha, in case Sgt. Carson would try to build a case against me? And something else just occurred to me. If it comes out that you knew I was involved and the thing happens, could you get in trouble for not stopping it?"

Sean said, "First, I will be doing everything I can to stop this from happening. If I cannot prevent the shooting, we do have a lot to start the investigation. At this point, only the three of us know how much I know about all this. As long as we keep it that way, I can just say that I had talked to you, and you were given some money to help out, but you did not know who all was involved. You turned the money over to me as evidence. I can say that I told you to leave the area to make sure that you could prove that you were not involved. I think that will settle that issue. I will also be able to turn in the money that is in evidence. Don't worry about me, you just need to make sure that you have proof that you were not in town when and if it does happen. Pictures, documents like hotel receipts and personal witnesses that you and your "so-called" friend were there would be good evidence. It would be good if you could meet a few couples while there to further establish your presence in Myrtle Beach. Get their names and addresses under some excuse, just in case we may need to contact them later. One last thing. You need to leave early enough to check into the hotel before the event happens. Time stamps on documents form what I call rock-solid alibis". Sean winked at Samantha and said, "are you sure you are good enough friends for this?"

Samantha said, "My friend Danny, who owns Smitty's Bar and Grill, did suggest that Preston could be a psychopath. I may need to rethink my decision to go with him to the beach". We all laughed and decided it was time for a glass of wine.

After we finished our wine, I said that I needed to go by the sniper's nest to drop off the rifle. Sean said he would talk to us tomorrow. When I got ready to leave, Samantha said that she wanted to go with me. I was not sure that was a good idea, but she said she would be my lookout, or in sniper's terms, my spotter.

I went to my apartment and got the rifle and brought it back to Samantha's house. I put on some plastic gloves that I had purchased. I then removed the firing pin and wiped my fingerprints from the gun. I did not clean the trigger or trigger guard. I did not know if Sgt. Carson's prints were on the trigger, but I hoped they were.

Before we left Samantha's house, I had another thought. I got some clear tape to put on the door leading to the roof. As I was leaving the loft, I went up the stairs to the roof and put the tape on the door. I placed it vertically over the top of the door so it would not be easily seen. I thought that I would tell Sean about it so if the shooting did occur, he could go check out that area to see if the shooter left any clues.

Samantha and I drove her car to downtown Sandton. We drove around the block that Cary's store was on twice to make certain that no one was in the area. It was just after 1:00 am, and the area was clear. We parked on the side of the building, where the Honda was supposed to be. It was not there. This was the first confirmation that this was a setup. I got out with the sniper's rifle and told Samantha to keep a lookout and call my phone if any other cars came in the area. I made my way to the back of the store and went up the stairs to the loft area. I carefully opened the door to the loft and shined my light to make certain that no one was up there. It was clear, so I walked over to the corner window and laid the rifle down on the floor.

I then rejoined Samantha, and we returned home. I told Samantha that the event, if it did happen, was to take place at 3:00 pm, so if we left for Myrtle Beach at 9:00 am we would have time to get set up at the hotel. We agreed to meet at 9:00 am.

CHAPTER 21

GOING TO MYRTLE BEACH

Promptly at 9:00 I knocked on Samantha's door. She was dressed to kill in a very expensive black suit with a scarf that added color. Her hair was pulled back that made her smile look like it was part of her outfit. I can never get used to catching my breath when I see her all dressed up. I told her she looked beautiful. She grinned and said, "are you trying to butter me up". All I could say was, "Maybe. Why are you dressed so elegantly". She said, "We are playing the part of a newly married couple, so we need to look the part".

We loaded up the car and got on the road. We did stop at a fast-food restaurant to get breakfast. After we finished our food, I said, "We need to talk. I am so sorry that I got you into this. This is not how I imagined things work out for us. When you first offered me a job doing some handyman work at your place, I was elated. When you offered the garage apartment, I could not believe my good fortune. I was somewhat intimidated by how attractive you were, but I thought I would work hard and hopefully not be too distracted by you to keep me from doing a good job on your house.

"As we began spending time together, I was afraid about your finding out my background and what I had been talking to Sgt. Carson about. The only thing was that I could not stop myself from being drawn to you". I paused for a moment to gather my thoughts.

Samantha broke in and said, "Preston, I never believed in love at first sight. But when you walked up on my porch, I had butterflies. I was as nervous as a teenage girl. I have to admit that I tried to fight it, but it did not work. I kept telling myself to be careful. I guess I had been careful all my life, but I began to sense that you were what I had been waiting for. Every moment with you just confirmed that this was meant to be. So don't apologize for anything. I am right where I want and need to be".

I tried to talk but was a little choked up. Finally, I said, "After we were working together, I realized that you were like a missing piece of a puzzle in my life. You completed the puzzle". She teared up and said that she had the exact same thought that she had found her missing puzzle piece.

I said, "Samantha, the problem is that I am a jobless man with a lot of baggage. You are a successful person with your whole life ahead of you. You deserve a lot more than I have to offer, not to mention this mess I am in now. We have only known each other a couple of months".

I started to continue, but she said, "Stop. What you are trying to do is who you are. A good, sensitive, lovable guy. But I don't want to hear any more. We are meant for each other, and you know it. We will get through this mess in front of us now. Then we will work through anything else we see ahead of us. I have waited my whole life for you. I think if the whole story were known, you came here to find me. Think about how we met and how we clicked right off. You know it as well as I do. Now, let's forget the past and talk about the future".

I found a place to pull the car over. She asked what I was doing. I said, "I can't stand not being able to look at you while we are talking. Do you really know what you are getting into? You are a counselor. What advice would you give someone that came to you and told this story?"

Samantha said, "If I had any brains or foresight, I would say run to him and never look back". I leaned over and kissed her. I could have continued that all day, but a car passed by, blew their horn and gave us a thumbs up.

We stopped kissing and I resumed talking, "Samantha, you are the missing puzzle piece of my life. I have just been wandering around while I was a sniper, and while I was doing engineering. I felt there was something missing. That something was you. I think I knew it the first time I met you. I know I don't have much to offer you, except my commitment to be with you for the rest of my life. That is the long way of my asking, Samantha, will you marry me? I know this is not a very romantic place or way to propose, but I do not want to go another mile without looking into your eyes and waiting for your answer".

Samantha said, "While this is a little unexpected, I would have said yes the first time I saw you. I would love nothing better that to spend the rest of my life with you". As you would expect we kissed again… a few times. We then realized we needed to get back on the road to Myrtle Beach. But now the elephant in the room was gone. We knew exactly where each other stood.

The rest of the drive to Myrtle Beach was like we were floating. The time passed quickly, and we arrived at the Grand Strand Hotel. We thought it looked like the best hotel in the area. It was just after 12:00 noon. We asked if they had a bridal suite, which they did. When the clerk asked our names, Samantha spoke up and said Mr. and Mrs. Preston Bourne. That sounded like music to my ears.

The clerk said normally check-in time was 3:00, but the suite was not in use, so he checked us in right away. After we got our luggage in the room, we looked around. It had a great view of the ocean. It was tastefully decorated the way you would expect a bridal suite.

I said," Samantha, please sit down. I would like to finish our conversation from the car. Based on what was said earlier, I would like to add some words to what I said. You said you would like to spend the rest of our lives together. Well, now before God, I promise to do everything I can to protect you, love you and be the best person I can and help you be the best person you can be, although you seem perfect now. I do not have a ring, but that will be rectified soon. From this day, I consider us married in every way. Paperwork will follow. However, I want you to know that I want you to have a real wedding. I want it to be everything you want it to be, wedding dress, bride maids and all the trimmings. I cannot imagine how I could be any happier. When we checked in and you said we were Mr. and Mrs. Preston Bourne, I wanted to start bawling there in the lobby. When all this other mess is over, I want a honeymoon that we will never forget".

Samantha said, "Preston, I also could not be any happier. I

do promise to be the best wife I can be. I want to be your helper and I will support you in all things. You are truly the answer to all my prayers, even some I did not know to pray for. As far as a real wedding as you called it, we will talk about that. For now, I would be satisfied if things stayed just the way they are, but we do have appearances to keep up. Like you, my promise is to you with God as my witness. I love you. We kissed, now in our minds as husband and wife.

I said, "It is just about 3 hours until the event in Sandton, if it does go ahead. What can we do until then? We are in the bridal suite.

According to Sean, we need to stay here for two or three days. I looked at Samantha and said, " You are the prettiest bride I have ever seen. Since this will be a short honeymoon, where would you like to go on our next honeymoon?"

CHAPTER 22

THE STRIKE

At 2:00 pm I decided to call Sean to see if anything was happening or if there was any news. Sean mentioned that he had a discussion with Sgt. Carson about the upcoming church announcement. Sean said that Carson seemed a little nervous, but there were not any indications that anything was wrong. Carson said that he would be going to Father Bishop's announcement at 3:00 pm. Carson said that the announcement was about the Catholic Church was going to build a boarding school in downtown Sandton. He said that he would be attending the ceremonies since he was friends with Father Bishop.

Sean said, "I have been by the sniper's nest early this morning and the rifle was still there. I checked the tape you put on the door to the roof, and it was still there. Based on this, it looks like there may not be a second shooter. I will be checking the area out for the possible sniper".

I said, "I hope that is the case. Be careful and call me after 3:00 pm to report". Samantha and I decided to go for a walk and hopefully to meet some people to establish our presence in Myrtle

Beach. We stopped by the hotel counter and talked to the clerk for a few minutes. We asked for a good seafood restaurant. She recommended Captain Shark's Seafood.

Before we left, I asked her the time. She said it was 2:30. I asked her name and if she lived in Myrtle Beach. She was very pleasant and said she had lived in Myrtle Beach her whole life. That was one witness. We wanted to get three or four more possible witnesses to our being in Myrtle Beach since some witnesses often get confused or don't remember details very well.

We walked down to the beach and saw a bar. We agreed it would be a good place to meet other people. We sat down at the bar and ordered a couple of fruity drinks. There was a couple sitting next to us, so we introduced ourselves. They told us they were Robert and Sue Kushner from Charlotte. We told them we were from Sandton. smiled and said, "Let me guess. You are newlyweds". Samantha and I looked at each other and smiled and said, "Yes," together. Samantha said, "How did not you know?" Sue said, "The sparkle in your eyes can only mean one of two things. Either you are newlyweds, or you are pregnant". Samantha said, "Your perception in amazing. I am certainly not pregnant. I am a counselor. I could use a gift like yours".

Sue said, "It is not really a gift. Looking at you two, it is pretty obvious. The real gift would be to be able to keep that look in your eyes for years to come. We said our pleasantries, left the bar, and continued our walk down the beach. We had not gone far, when I received a call from Sean.

Preston answered the phone on the first ring. Sean excitedly said, "Preston, it just happened. The crowd is running in all directions. TV cameras are everywhere. At few minutes ago a shot took Father Bishop out. Sgt. Carson shouted to his Lieutenant, who just happened to be a member of Father Bishop's church, that he saw what looked like a muzzle fire from the top of Cary's store. Carson immediately ran over there. He said he saw someone running away from the loft area but could not keep up with the runner. Strangely enough, Carson's description sounded very much like you. He obviously did not get a look at the runner's face. I hope you have established your alibis sufficiently.

The investigation will begin soon. As we discussed earlier, I think you should stay in Myrtle Beach for a few days. At this point, Sgt. Carson cannot name you as a suspect. He does not have any evidence. All he could say was that he talked to a guy that was a Marine sniper. Bottom line, nothing to worry about at this time. Stay down there and have fun".

I said, "Sean, there is a new development. Samantha and I are a number now. Not like dating, something much deeper. No paperwork, but ...".

There is something else. I think the other three guys will be needing to get together soon. I have GPS-tractors on William Jameson's and Sgt. Carson's cars. I think we need to cut our honeymoon short and get back to Sandton so I can tract both of them. If they get together again, we need to know that. I wish we had a way to hear their conversation. Do you have any ideas? We will leave Myrtle Beach tomorrow morning". Sean said he understood and agreed.

I looked at Samantha and said, "I hate to do this. I imagine you heard most of the conversation". Samantha nodded and said,

"I agree completely, but this will not function as our honeymoon. I assume you understand that".

I said, "I would be an idiot to pass up a chance to have a honeymoon with you. In fact, when we get past this hurdle, we will do the honeymoon in grand style, assuming I can get an advance from my employer". We both grinned. We decided to find the great seafood restaurant and to start our short honeymoon over again. We agreed that Sandton did not need any more of our time until we got back home. Looking into her eyes, I saw some of what Sue Kushner had seen in her eyes and I agreed completely.

CHAPTER 23

RETURNING TO SANDTON

Just lying there watching Samantha sleep, I knew we were both right, that it was the time for both of us. We were right for each other. Or at least she was right for me. I hoped I could eventually prove I was right for her.

When she woke up, we got our things together and checked out. We told the hotel desk clerk that we really enjoyed the short time at their hotel, but we had an emergency and had to return home. We got on the road by 8:30 am and thought we would be back in Sandton before lunch. We both thought that the three guys would want to get together soon. We just hoped that they had not already had their meeting. We also hoped that they would not try to have their meeting over the phone.

We called Sean and told him we were on the way. He said he was able to find a listening device at the police station that could pick up conversations through windows or glass doors. That sounded like our only option. I asked about a directional microphone that would allow us to filter out background noises. He said he would check to see if they had one at the station. He added that when we got back to Sandton, that we should let him know if we see movement of both the tracking devices. He said that since the investigation was underway now, it would be best if he went along with us when we were doing anything associated with the investigation.

We arrived back in Sandton a few minutes before noon. I checked my GPS tracking app and saw that both cars were stationary. Sgt. Carson was at the police station and William Jameson was at home. We assumed that Sgt. Carson was at the police station working on the investigation. It occurred to me that I should ask Sean what Sgt. Carson's involvement in the investigation was.

Sean called and said he had found a directional microphone that we could use. This got all three of us excited, even though we did not know how we could get close enough to use it. I asked Sean about Sgt. Carson's involvement in the investigation. He said that this was a reasonably small town and investigations like this do not come along very often. That means everyone in the police department wanted to get involved in some way. He added that he did not see any problems there.

I said, "My concern is about him knowing what we were doing and that he may be able to interfere with our efforts".

Sean said that his efforts with us would not be part of the investigation record. Although Sean had seemed to be straight with us, I had my doubts that Sgt. Carson would not be able to find out about Samantha and me.

This started me thinking again about whether I should keep my distance from Samantha until this matter is settled. I decided to wait about mentioning this until Samantha, Sean and I got together. I felt like I knew what Samantha would say, but I wanted to get Sean's input before we made any decision that could endanger Samantha.

Our process now became that of finding evidence of who all the people were that had been involved in the shooting death of Father Bishop. We had to figure out how to get evidence that would hold up in court. Samantha and I were glad that we had been working with Sean. Not only could he assist us in gathering the evidence, but he would also be able to evaluate how well it would stand up in court. About the only thing we would be able to be involved in would be to use the GPS units to track the movement of Carson and Jameson. We called Sean and set up 2:00 pm to meet at Samantha's house to figure out how we would begin to gather evidence.

While we were waiting for Sean, I said, "Do you realize that in the last two months, we met, I started working on your house, we dated a few times and we are now married, although not with the official wedding ceremony? What will the next two months hold for us?"

Samantha said, "Hopefully, this investigation will be behind us, and we can have our real honeymoon. You do remember your promise of a real honeymoon, right?"

I grinned and responded, "Believe me, there is no way I would ever forget our upcoming honeymoon. There is one fly in the ointment. How are you going to tell your friend Danny that we are married? I cannot imagine that he will be very happy with you marrying an unemployed bum after only knowing me for only a couple of months".

Samantha grinned and said, " You know I told you Danny was like a big brother and even sometimes like a father. So, I think that means it is you that have to ask him for my hand in marriage". She watched me squirm for a few seconds, then said, "Actually, we are going to have a marriage ceremony a few months from now, so I suggest we just not mention that we are already married, just not officially. We will not give him any reason to think that things have changed. I would prefer to shout to the world that we are married, but better judgement says wait". I think she could see the relief in my face. Thankfully, Sean arrived and took me off the hot seat.

I told Sean that both cars that I had installed GPS tracking devices on were still stationary. Sean said that if Sgt. Carson's car left the police station, we should follow it in case he chose to meet the shooter. That thought had not occurred to me, but it was logical that the shooter would be expecting to get paid. So much had happened, it was hard to remember that the shooting occurred yesterday and that today was only Saturday.

Sean said that if both cars started to move, we would need to see if they were going in the same direction. He also said that we needed to figure out how we would use the sound listening device and the directional mike. He reiterated that just listening to them meeting together was not evidence of a crime. He also said that even if we could hear some of their conversation and they mentioned the shooting, which would likely not be admissible in court, without a court order to listen in on their conversation.

That would have to be determined later by a judge. However, we may gain some useful information if we can actually hear what they are saying.

He said, "If they happen to meet in a restaurant and sit near a window, we may be able to pick up their conversation. If they are not near a window, we may have to come up with a way to go in the restaurant and use the directional microphone. Both of these options are long shots".

I spoke up, "Long shots are my specialty. What if you question one of the three men about their involvement in the shooting? If you chose the weakest link, he might give us the evidence we need". The best one is William Jameson, the Chairman of the City Council. He has the most to lose and was likely not directly involved with the shooter".

I continued, "Sgt. Carson has a lot to lose, but is likely the toughest nut to crack of all three. I do think this should be our last-ditch effort if we cannot get any evidence any other way". We all agreed. We decided our main effort would be to follow them if it looked like they were planning to meet.

Samantha spoke up, "What about getting fingerprints off the gun?" Sean said that it was being kept in the evidence lockup area. He added that since he was the detective in charge, he would be the one to request checking fingerprints on the gun. Sean also added, "After I submit the request for fingerprint testing, I will get a statement from Sgt. Carson about how careful he was when he picked up the gun in the shooter's nest. I feel sure he will say he was very careful, hoping to find some of the shooter's prints on the rifle. Since I am the requesting officer for the fingerprint report, it will be sent to me. I will request that the technician not share information in the report with anyone while the investigation is underway. I feel sure that the technician will find some of my prints on the rifle, and since I have not been in possession of the rifle, they should not be on the rifle. The technician will not know that I have not handled the rifle after the shooting.

"There is one thing I do not want you to get your hopes on. If Sgt. Carson says he was very careful about what he touched on the rifle, and his prints show up on the trigger, he would likely just say he must have inadvertently touched is when he picked up the rifle in the shooter's nest. Since I will be the one with the fingerprint report, I can tell Sgt. Carson that there are other fingerprints on the rifle that I will be running through the data bases to determine who has handled the rifle.

"This should make him relax, thinking that it is your prints, Preston that are found on the rifle and that I will be searching the data bases to find. I feel sure he will suggest my running it through military records, since he knows that you are a past marine sniper".

CHAPTER 24

THE INVESTIGATION CONTINUES

On Monday, Sean called and asked if he could come over. He said that he thought it would be best if Samantha were not there because he needed to have an investigation type discussion for the record. He said that the investigation was in full swing now, so he needed to get a statement from me.

Sean arrived in 30 minutes, and we decided to meet in my apartment. Sean began, "Before we start the questions, please answer them as if we have not met or been working together. This interview and the notes I take will be reviewed by others so I think this meeting should follow normal procedures. Do you understand what I am saying, and do you mind if I record our conversation?" I responded that I thought I did understand, and I did not mind his recording the discussion. Something seemed different about Sean, but I told him to go ahead.

"Hello Mr. Bourne. I am Detective Murphy. I am looking into the shooting of Father Bishop. Do you mind if I record our conversation?" I said he could record our conversation. He turned the recorder on and continued, "This is a terrible thing. Did you know him?"

I said, "No Detective, I never met him. By the way, call me Preston. I have only been in South Carolina for two or three months and I am not Catholic, so I would not have met him. I am curious why you wanted to see me though. Is it because I am new in town?"

"Well, Mr. Bourne, uh Preston, our city is not that large, and we normally have very little crime. Certainly, when something like this happens, we start scratching our heads and wondering what has changed in our city. Naturally, we do wonder what brings new people here. However, to be honest I am following up on something an anonymous tipper sent to us, and I thought you might be able to help me out".

"Well, Detective, I'm not sure how I can help, but I will help you in any way I can. I have heard about the case from the news reports on TV. There does not seem to be a lot of information at this point. Do you have any suspects yet?"

Mr. Bourne, very little is known at this time and since it is a current investigation, I am limited on what I can say about it. First, could you tell me about yourself? Where you came from, what brought you to Sandton, just background information. You say you have been here only a couple of months? What kind of work do you do?"

"I came here from Oklahoma. I just wanted to start over, and I heard a lot of good things about your state and your city in particular. I just sold my house and moved here".

"Preston, we like to think we have the best place in the world to live. That is until something like this past week's crime. We have never had anything like this happen here. That is why we have to follow up on each and every lead we get".

"Detective, this is all interesting, but you are not here from the Chamber of Commerce. You are a police detective. Why are you here? Do you think I am involved in the shooting of the Catholic Priest?"

"I understand, Preston, sometimes we policemen tend to get bogged down in background information. Actually, I am here because I got a tip, or video I should say that I would like you to help me with. In the video, you were identified receiving a paper bag from an unidentified person in what look like suspicious circumstances. I just wanted to follow-up on this and hear what you had to say about it".

Detective, can I see the video? Maybe I can shed some light on it. This all sounds a little bazar".

"Preston, this is a little unusual for me to share this video with you, but under the circumstances, I would like to hear you explanation. Let's watch it on my phone and then you can tell me what you know about this".

"After watching the video, Detective, I have to admit that is me receiving the bag. What doesn't show up very well is what I handed the other person. The person that recorded the video did a good job of capturing my image but did not get any shots of the person that gave me the bag. Also, I have a couple of questions. First, how did you determine that was me in the video? I have not been here long and do not know very many people. Second, who sent you the video? Is it someone I know?"

"Preston, I am not accusing you of anything. I just wanted to follow-up on what the person that sent the video thought was suspicious behavior. While this video was taken in a public restaurant which does not make it suspicious, the person that sent it thought it was and thought it could be connected to the shooting".

"I am sorry Detective; I don't want to be uncooperative. It's just that I don't believe in coincidences. It seems strange that someone thought it so unusual for one person to hand another person a paper bag in a public restaurant that they would video the meeting. Also, watch the video again. Note when the video starts. Do you see that the video started before I met the stranger that came up to my table? How did the person shooting the video know that there would be something suspicious happening? As I said, I do not believe in coincidences. Since I am relatively new in town, I ask you again, how did you identify that it was me in the video so quickly?

"Preston, this is an ongoing investigation, so I cannot reveal some details at this time".

"Detective, you just showed me the video. How is that not revealing details? It seems that the only details you guys won't reveal are the details that could disprove what is already made up in your minds. You come here asking me stupid questions about what you say is suspicious behavior. Why don't you just ask me what is really on your mind?" Detective Murphy did not answer. He just stared at me.

After a few seconds, I said, "I am sorry Detective, this is frustrating since it does not make any sense. I know you are only doing your job. Yes, that is me in the video. Let me explain something. Have you ever heard of Craigslist? Well, I had some software that I no longer needed, so I put it on Craigslist. I am not destitute, but I have not found permanent employment yet so I thought I could clean up my apartment by getting rid of things I don't need any more and make a little money at the same time".

Detective Murphy scratched his cheek as if he understood and was unsure of where to go next. "Preston, what software were you selling? Can you prove you were trying to sell things? The video did show that you handed something to the other person. What was that?"

"I actually sold three pieces of software. Windows 7, Microsoft Office 16 and AutoCad 16. I had them on a thumb drive. You can see that in the video".

"Preston, I know about the first two, but what is AutoCad 16? And how much did you get for the software?"

I said, "AutoCad 16 is a program used in the engineering industry to make drawings for chemical plants. That is what I used to do, design chemical plants. But I do not need it now. I have newer versions of the other software. I was asking $400 for all three pieces of software, but you seldom get what you ask for. We finally settled for $300. I told the gentleman that I would have to have cash. He said that would be fine.

"We agreed to meet at the Sandton Steak House at 4:00 pm on Friday as I recall. Well, he showed up at exactly 4:00 as planned. He had the money in a paper bag and when I opened the bag, it had a bunch of one-dollar bills. Normally, I would have counted the money, but since we were in a restaurant, I did not think it would be good to have three hundred one dollar bills out in the open. I gave him the software and we parted.

"I felt odd with the bag of money, so I walked down Broad Street to my bank, since it was only two blocks away.

"I was a little embarrassed when I handed the bag of one-dollar bills to Cindy at the bank. I mentioned that I hated to trouble her, but she said the machine behind her would count it out in a few seconds. I deposited the $300 in my account and left".

"Preston, I think I understand the video better now. Two questions, do you still have the deposit slip from the bank, and do you know the name of the man who bought the software?"

I replied, "The answer to the first question is yes. I keep all my deposit slips for one year. You never know when they may come in handy. And as to the man's name, he only introduced himself as Jimmy. He said he did not have a phone number that is working now and had to borrow a friend's phone to call me. It sounded a little strange, but you meet some strange people on these merchandise web sites. Let me get you the deposit slip". I got up and went to my bedroom to my chest of drawers. I returned to my den and handed the deposit slip to Detective Murphy.

"Preston, I appreciate your being so forth coming and taking the time to fill in all the details of your transaction. And I see that the deposit slip is for $300, and the time stamp is at 4:32 pm on Friday the 4th. Do you mind if I keep this for a couple of days? I will return it to you. One thing seems a little strange. Why did you deposit all the money and not keep a little for spending money?"

"Well, Detective, have you ever walked around with a wad of one-dollar bills in your pocket? It kind of makes a lump in your pocket and will not fit in your wallet. Besides, I had twenty or thirty dollars in my billfold, so I did not need any more. It was just easier to keep up with it in the bank account.

"Detective, before you go, I would like to ask you again. What would anyone think two guys meeting in a restaurant exchanging a paper bag for software and going separate ways was suspicious? And I still want to know why it appears that the video started before the other man came up to my table. Why would make whoever made that video start it when I was sitting at the table by myself?"

"Preston, I agree. I had the same thoughts. I am impressed that you picked up on that detail".

"Well, detective, I am an engineer. I was paid to pay attention to details. Also, I failed to mention that I was a Marine sniper in Afghanistan. Paying attention to details is why I am still alive".

"Preston, I understand what you have shared with me, and it makes sense. I am sorry to have taken up so much of your time. You said you are not an engineer anymore. What are you doing now?"

"Not sure yet detective, just reevaluating things. But I still want to know how you identified me in the video so quickly. I do not know many people in Sandton".

"Preston, I probably should not tell you this, but I think you know Sgt. Carson. He saw the video and recognized you. You didn't hear that from me".

"Sure, I know Sgt. Carson. We met at Casey's Bar a few times. He said he knew I must be new in town since he did not recognize me. He seemed like a nice guy. You know Detective, with the timing of the video starting, I believe I would concentrate on finding who sent the video. It almost looks like a setup, but for what?

"Preston, the person that gave us the tip and video said they thought the two of you looked suspicious and that the bag could be payoff for the murder of the priest".

"So, I am a suspect in the murder of the priest that I had never met. This is in incredible. I repeat, I think whoever took the video and sent it to you should answer a few questions. By the way, who did the "source" sent the video to?"

"Preston, I agree with what you are saying. I will be trying to track the source of the video down. The video was delivered to the front desk at the police station and was addressed to "whoever is investigating the murder of Father Bishop". You know Preston, I just hate it when I leave an interview with more questions than I had when I arrived. Since there are so many new questions, I may need to talk to you again. You are not planning on leaving town, are you?"

I replied, "How could I leave? This is just getting more interesting by the minute".

Sean turned off the recorder and said, "Okay, Preston, the interview is over. I appreciate the way you handled the questions and your other input. I think it is good, since the others reviewing the taped interview will get a chance to know a little more about you, information I have learned in the short time I have known you. But there is one other thing Preston that I feel I must mention. The thought popped into my mind, as I am sure it will into the minds of other officers reviewing the taped interview. I really hate to bring it up, but I need to ask anyway. Could you have brought me into your circle to cover up that you were actually involved in the murder of Father Bishop either in the shooting or planning?"

I smiled and said, "I would have to admit that would have been a gutsy thing to do, but maybe also smart. It is understandable that line of thought could come up. However, Sean based on my background as a sniper, I would not even consider having anything to do with the police. With my sniper training, if I had done the shooting, I would have been long gone within minutes after the shot was fired. I would not be alive today if I were not good at disappearing in much more difficult situations than this. Also, don't forget that it was you that suggested that I establish a "rock-solid" alibi.

Sean said, " I agree with what you have said. We will talk tomorrow. Keep an eye on the GPS trackers". He started to leave but turned around and smiled. He said, "Are you really smart enough to have plotted out all the things like the firing pin on the rifle, the GPS tracking devices and the money exchange in the restaurant?" I just smiled and said, "See you tomorrow".

CHAPTER 25

DETAILS, DETAILS, DETAILS

When Sean got back to the police station, he asked the desk clerk about the video package. "Were you on duty when the video package came?" Officer Young said that he did receive the package. Sean asked, "How was it delivered? Was it USPS, UPS or FedEx, and did you have to sign anything?"

Officer Young looked confused, thought for a minute and then said, "It was USPS, and I did have to sign a receipt slip. He opened a drawer behind the desk, rummaged around it and handed Detective Murphy the receipt. I hope this helps," he said.

Murphy replied that it was probably a needle in a haystack, but it was better than no clue. When he got back to his office, he made a list of things to follow-up on:

1. Call the post office to determine if the signed receipt would help identify who sent the video package.
2. Follow-up on that information if the post office had any information.

3. Rewatch the video to determine exactly when the video started and who it focused on first.
4. Do a background check on Preston.
5. Talk to Sgt. Carson to see what he knows about Preston.
6. Talk to Cindy at Preston's bank to see if she remembers anything about the transaction.

Murphy was reviewing his list and mumbling to himself when Sgt. Carson stepped into his office.

"Detective, are you okay? This case isn't getting you down, is it?"

"Yeah, Sgt. Carson. This is a puzzling case. But since we don't get many murders in Sandton, I guess I am out of practice. By the way, do you have a few minutes? I have some questions about Preston Bourne".

"Sure Detective, what do you need to know?

"First off, you mentioned that the two of you had met several times at Casey's Bar and had a few drinks. I talked to him for a few minutes, and he remembered meeting you. Did he tell you about his background? Where he came from, why he moved here, why he gave up his job, etc.?"

Yes, at first, he didn't talk much about his past, but the second or third times we ran into each other at the bar, he began to open up after a few drinks. He is a complicated person. I asked him what he did in Texas. That is where he is from".

"Sgt. Carson let me get clarification on what he told me. He said he was from Oklahoma. You say he is from Texas?"

"Actually, Detective you are correct. At first, he said he moved here from Texas, but he later said his home was in Oklahoma, but he built a chemical plant in Texas. He owned an engineering firm and had designed a chemical plant somewhere in Texas. He spent a lot of time at the plant during construction. When I asked what he was doing here, he clammed up. He left the bar shortly after that".

"The next time we met he began to explain why he left Texas and Oklahoma. When the plant was up and running, he returned to Oklahoma. After a few months, one of the men that was operating the plant was killed by one of the pieces of equipment. The incident was investigated, and his company was cleared of any wrongdoing. It was a simple case of operator error. So legally, the matter was over.

"However, it apparently got to his head. The operator that died had a wife and two children. They did not have much money and very little life insurance. It bothered Mr. Bourne so much that he sold his company and house and moved here. He apparently gave the family the money from his business and house. He did not want to talk about it anymore. I did not probe any further. As the night went on, we had a few more drinks and he started talking about being in the armed forces, special forces or something like that. Again, he did not go into details, so I let it drop. He seemed to me to be somewhat troubled. Can't put my finger on it, but something just seems off".

"Sgt. Carson, if you happen to meet for drinks again, see what else you can find out about his background. Does he have a wife, kids, that sort of thing. As I said, I met with him about the video, but he seemed to have a plausible explanation for the circumstances on the video. I have a few items to check on what he told me, but he doesn't seem like a strong contender to be a suspect. Unfortunately, he is the only one we have.

I will do a little checking on his military background, as well as, why he gave up owning an engineering business and now does not even have a job as an engineer. I am wondering how much money he has and how he is paying for living expenses".

After Sgt. Carson left his office, Murphy decided to make a couple of stops. First, he would go to the bank to talk to Cindy. Then he would go by the post office to see what information he could find out about the sender of the delivered package.

When Murphy entered the bank, he saw Max Harper, the bank manager. After they exchanged some small talk about their families, Murphy asked if he could talk to Cindy about a past transaction. Max looked at the teller windows and did not see Cindy. He said she must be on break, and he would find her. He smiled and said, "You are not here to arrest her are you?"

Murphy smiled back and said that he only needed to talk to her about a deposit someone had made and the circumstances around the deposit. He further explained that Cindy had handled the transaction.

Max left to find Cindy and returned with Cindy in tow in a couple of minutes. Murphy and Cindy went into one of the vacant offices. Murphy began, "Cindy you may not remember the transaction in question, but it concerns Mr. Preston Bourne". Cindy perked up. "Yes, I know Mr. Bourne. He is a very pleasant man. Very polite. What questions do you have? What is this about? Mr. Bourne is not in any trouble, is he?"

Murphy broke in, "No, Cindy, there was just a question about a recent deposit he made. He said he recently deposited $300 in his account. Do you recall him making that deposit?"

"Yes, Detective, he was very apologetic about depositing three hundred one-dollar bills. He thought it would be a lot of trouble for me to have to count the money. I explained that we have a machine that counts it for us".

"Cindy, did he give you an explanation about why he was depositing that many one-dollar bills?"

Cindy responded that they had a good laugh about it. "I mean three hundred one-dollar bills in a brown paper bag is a little out of the ordinary. Mr. Bourne said he had just sold some computer software and the guy paid him with the three hundred one-dollar bills. He mentioned that he hoped it was all there, because he had not been able to count it. I told him not to worry, the machine will tell us exactly how much is in the paper bag. Sure enough, it was all there, so we completed the deposit and he left".

"Cindy, is there anything else odd about the transaction?"

"No, Detective, that is pretty much all that was said, except he thanked me for my patience and assistance".

"Cindy, can you tell me how much money Mr. Bourne has in his account?"

"No, Detective, we cannot give out information about a customer's account without their written permission. Sorry".

"That's okay Cindy, I understand. You have been very helpful, and no, Mr. Bourne is not in any trouble".

As Murphy left the bank, his main thought was that all Preston had said was true. He truly did not believe that Preston had anything to do with the murder but the police in him would not let him follow the urge to eliminate Preston as a suspect. From what he knew about Preston, he just seemed to be too honest, and too normal to be involved in this or any other criminal case.

Murphy had just enough time to get to the post office before they closed. While walking to the post office, his thoughts kept going back to how important it was to establish who sent the video. He knew it was a long shot. If the person were attempting to frame Preston, it would be doubtful that they would make an amateur mistake that could be traced back to them. It was possible the person that took the video truly thought the restaurant meeting was suspicious, and they were trying to be helpful. However, it didn't make sense that they wouldn't identify themselves.

When he entered the post office, he saw that there was a long line of people trying to take care of business before closing time. He walked over to one postal agent he recognized and asked to see the shift supervisor. Because of the crowd, the supervisor invited Murphy back to her office. After perfunctory introductions, Murphy explained that the police department received a package and had to sign for it. What he wanted to know was if the post office would have a record of who sent it.

The supervisor, Ms. Wilson, said that since the package required a signature the sender would be required to sign the paperwork. She looked at the receipt from the police department and confirmed that there would be a signature on file. However, the only problem was that the package was not sent from Sandton's post office. The office code was for the post office in Brandenburg. Ms. Wilson asked Murphy if he would like her to request a copy of the paperwork from the Brandenburg post office.

Murphy thanked her but said that he preferred to go pick up the form himself. He did ask for the office manager's name and contact information. He thanked her again and left.

Murphy couldn't help feeling a little excited that the sender would have had to sign the form to send the package. The thing that tempered his excitement was that the person had taken the video in Sandton but had sent the video to the Sandton police department from Brandenburg. It seems that nothing is ever easy in his cases.

CHAPTER 26

PATH FORWARD

On Wednesday, Sean called and asked if Samantha and I could meet with him at Samantha's house. We agreed to meet at noontime and have lunch. Samantha and I made some ham and cheese sandwiches. Lunch would not be complete without Samantha's lemonade.

When Sean arrived, we sat down to eat lunch. He looked at his paper towel napkin and said, "What, no linen napkins. I must be pretty far down on your list of important people". Samantha said, "It depends on what information you have for us. If it is good, the linen will come out for dessert. If it is not good, this is as good as it gets".

Sean said, "Well, I think Preston may be innocent. Does that count as good? I checked with Cindy at the bank and her story matches Preston's story. I followed up on the video we received at the police station. It was recorded at the Sandton Steak House. It was sent from the Brandenburg post office. I got the name of the person who sent it. His name was George Brown. My guess is that may not be his or her real name. I did get the signed receipt from the post office to check for fingerprints, but I do not hold out much hope for success in that area. In summary, I guess our dessert will be with paper towel napkins. At this point, I think we have three paths forward. Number one is to watch the GPS units and see if Sgt. Carson meets with the potential shooter again. We can then follow the potential shooter and then decide what to do about him.

"I had an idea about what we might be able to do. If we are lucky and there is a warrant out for his arrest, we can take him into custody. We can then try to get a search warrant for his trailer and hope we find something linking him to the shooting and therefore to Sgt. Carson. That would give us reason to arrest all three of the other men. Hopefully, one of them will crack in questioning.

"If we do not find a warrant out on the potential shooter, option number two is to watch the GPS units for a meeting of the three men. If they do meet and we can get some information from the listening devices, we can then maybe arrest the three men and the potential shooter. Again, we really need one of them to break under questioning. The third path is to simply arrest the three men and hope one of them breaks under questioning. The only other thing I can think of is to hope that the fingerprints on the rifle turns up something".

Preston said, "I am thinking out loud. What could you ask Sgt. Carson that would make him want to get the other two guys together so we could follow them and possibly eavesdrop on them?"

Samantha spoke up, "What if you tell Sgt. Carson you heard a rumor that the City Council was going to refuse to give Bishop's church a permit to build the school in that building downtown?

Do you think he would panic and want to know what that was about?"

Both Preston and Sean smiled and simultaneously said great idea.

Sean said, "That would surely make Sgt. Carson want to get together with William Jameson, the Chairman of the City Council. Not sure if Jerry Truman would show up for the meeting, but I can imagine that Sgt. Carson would want to go into damage control if he thought that Jameson and Father Bishop had argued about the proposed school. Carson could think that the investigation team might think that there was a conflict of interest or something that linked the two men together.

"We still have a problem that we may not be able to pick up their conversation. We cannot plant a bug on them because we have no way to know what clothes they may wear if they do get together".

While we were thinking about how to get access to their conversation, if it every happened, Sgt. Carson's car and William Jameson's car both started to move. The three of us looked at each other in surprise. We said let's go. We decided to go in Samantha's car. I thought to get my bag of disguises in case I needed them. After a few minutes, it was apparent that they both were heading toward Brandenburg. Samantha said let's hope they go to a restaurant with a large picture window.

I asked Sean, "What conversation could they have to give you reason to arrest them?" He replied, "Unless they outright admit being involved in the murder, the best we could hope for is that they say something that would lead us to a real clue. Without that,

I am afraid we are back to square one, unless Sgt. Carson leads us to the shooter".

I spoke up and said, "There is one other option we have not discussed. What if I call Sgt. Carson and tell him we need to meet? He will surely agree to meet with me. I could wear a wire and try to get him to explain why he had a back-up shooter. He would have to ask me why I took the money and did not go through with the job. I could keep asking why a back-up shooter. He obviously would have to say something".

Samantha almost screamed, "Are you crazy? He won't answer your questions, he will shoot you immediately. He would then make up a story about you going for a gun and that he reacted in self-defense. I could see him starting to shoot the minute you get out of your car".

I was about ready to respond when both cars pulled into the Sundown Motel parking lot. Luckily, the motel had rooms with doors on the outside walkway. It appeared that someone had arrived earlier and got a room since both men did not go to the office to get a room key. We assumed that Jerry Truman must have arrived earlier and had secured a room. Both Sgt. Carson and William Jameson got out of their cars and went up to the second floor to room 215.

Sean already had the listening device out and was setting it up pointing at the window in room 215. Unfortunately, the drapes were closed and that muffled the sound from the room. They had to stay near their car in case one or all three of the men came out of the room.

What we could hear was someone raising his voice. A second

voice jumped in almost shouting. We made out the words, "What in the hell were you thinking? This is not what we were talking about". We made out those words because whoever was talking was shouting. The problem was, we did not know who was talking or what they were talking about. The remainder of the conversation was back to being muffled.

In a couple of minutes, the door opened, and William Jameson stormed out and slammed the door behind him. Sgt. Carson and Jerry Truman did not leave immediately.

Sean spoke up and said, "I think we have found the weakest link. If we have to try to get one of them to break down, I think it will be Jameson. It will still be very risky. If he lawyers up immediately, we may get nothing and will alarm the others". We returned to Samantha's house to talk about what we had learned tonight.

I spoke up and said, "Based on what we did not hear from the motel room, I think we are down to my calling Sgt. Carson and setting up a meeting". Samantha started shaking her head, but I put up my hand and said, "We at least need to discuss this option. We can pick a public place and I can wear a wire. Sean can be close by ready to act. There has to be a way to do this to minimize the danger".

Sean spoke up, "I agree with Samantha. I think it is too dangerous. Even in a public place, he could pick his time to shoot you and say you were a danger to the public". I said, "Okay, we will shelve this for now, but we need to keep it in mind. I could even wear a bullet-proof vest. There is an old saying, 'Fore-warned is fore-armed' or something like that. Remember, I am a Marine, trained in special forces, or as they say in Texas, 'this is not my first rodeo.'

"I finally said that we have done all we can for now. We can keep each other up to date if there are any new developments". We agreed to talk tomorrow, and Sean left.

Samantha and I had a tough day, so we decided it was time for a glass or two of wine. When we sat down, Samantha looked at me and said, "Preston, I cannot lose you now, even if those who killed Father Bishop get away with it. You are my world now. Please do not do anything that puts you in danger. Promise me that you will do what I ask". I looked into her eyes and was reminded that the eyes are the doorway to a person's soul. I could see the deep concern in her eyes. Tears came to my eyes, and I simply said, "I promise".

We sat there holding each other for a long time without saying a word. It felt as if we could stay there forever. I finally said, let's go to bed. She grinned and said, "my place or yours". She then said that actually both my place and yours are 'ours'.

CHAPTER 27

A BREAK IN THE CASE

The next morning, we awoke to a beautiful day. It was a perfect day even though yesterday had not been a good day of investigation. The men's meeting of the conspirators had not given us any concrete information that would be useful in getting to the bottom of the murder case. But the time that Samantha and I had spent together along with having wine in 'our' place just seemed so natural. It is amazing that two people can just embrace each other without saying anything, and the world seems to be without worries, troubles, or disasters. The intimacy that follows, is the final piece of the puzzle for a world at peace.

After breakfast, we realized that we did not have any investigative work to do, unless the GPS-trackers indicated that we needed to follow one or both cars. When I turned the GPS trackers on, the cars actually went where they would normally go. Since we did not have anything that needed doing, we decided to ride bikes, walk in the woods and just stay close to home.

We had to be ready to go if the GPS-tracking devices indicated cars on the move. It turned out to be a day of spending time together with nothing pulling us away from enjoying each other and the great day.

We thought about going out to eat but realized that we had to stay within range of the GPS units. I also had to be careful not to be seen by Sgt. Carson. As much as we hated to, we got take-out from a restaurant and ate dinner at home. Nothing happened on the GPS units until about 9:30 that night. Sgt. Carson's car began to leave his apartment going south. I jumped in Samantha's car, and she naturally jumped in and would not consider staying behind. I was driving, so Samantha called Sean and told him we were following Sgt. Carson. She told him where we were, and he said he would join us. It appeared that we were going in the direction of the deserted bowling alley where Sgt. Carson had met the shooter before.

I told Sean to go past the bowling alley to a warehouse parking lot just past the bowling alley. That is where Samantha and I were going to park, so it would look like some people were at the warehouse working. Sgt. Carson pulled into the bowling alley parking lot. We passed the bowling alley like before and pulled into the warehouse parking lot near the office a few seconds later. Sean arrived at the warehouse parking lot a couple of minutes later. We told him that Sgt. Carson was in the bowling alley parking lot, but no one else had arrived yet. We chose to stay in the car until whoever was meeting him arrived in the bowling alley parking lot. It was about 5 minutes later when another person driving a Ram truck pulled into the lot where Carson was parked.

As before when they met in the bowling alley parking lot, their cars were parked in opposite directions so that the driver's windows were next to each other. We got out hurriedly and went to the shrubs separating the two parking lots. Sean had brought the directional microphone so we could hear their conversation clearly, and also record it. The other man asked Sgt. Carson how the investigation was going. Sgt. Carson said, "not much had happened yet. The detective did have a conversation with the marine sniper, but he did not get anything useful. I sent the video of you meeting the sniper in the restaurant and you giving him the bag of money. By the way, what did he hand you?"

The other man said, "that was the darndest thing. He gave me a thumb drive or USB drive, whatever you call it. It was empty, but he said that it had the software on it. What do you think he did that for? I just took it and left, not wanting to make anyone notice us. How did the video come out? I was careful not to show my face".

Sgt. Carson said, "I do not know what he was up to when he handed you the thumb drive. The video was great. I went by the detective's office, and he showed me the video. I looked surprised and said, 'I know that guy'. He is the Marine sniper I told you about. The detective seemed pleased that I had recognized him. I gave him the sniper's phone number. He did follow-up with him. I have not read his report of his meeting, but I will get a chance in the next few days. I know he did send the rifle to have it checked for fingerprints, but I do not know when that report will be back. I sure hope there will be some prints somewhere on the gun. He did say that the fingerprint guy said there some prints on the rifle, but it will take some time to get confirmation from the Marines that the prints on the gun are his. How much longer do you plan to stay in the area?"

The other man said, "I will not be leaving until I get the final payment. When I get that, I will be moving on to take a vacation. How do I know you are not going to shoot me and pin the shooting on me instead of on the Marine? I was thinking you could just shoot me and say that you had captured the shooter and not have to pay me the final payment. I hope you do not have any thoughts like that. I am always keeping my guns handy. Just remember, I took one man out. I could just as easy take you out with the same sniper rifle".

Sgt. Carson said, "I want this investigation to end with the Marine blamed as much as you do. Actually, I have your final payment now. We have the perfect solution to this case in the Marine. I do have to locate him, but I will find him. I know his car and he does not know many people in Sandton. He will turn up. I also have his phone number and I will keep trying to reach him".

Sgt. Carson handed something, presumably the final payment, to the other man through the windows. The other man did not even bother to count it. He cranked his car. Sgt. Carson said, "aren't you going to count it?" The other man just laughed and said, "I do not think you would short the man who just killed a man for you. Remember, I just shot the priest and did not leave a single clue. I could do the same with you. Anyway, I am a trusting man, right?" With that, the other man pulled out of the parking lot. Sgt. Carson cranked his car and left in the opposite direction.

We stayed hidden in the bushes until the other man's car had left the parking lot. We got into Samantha's car and went to follow the other man. He drove for about 5 minutes to the trailer park I had followed him to before. We pulled into the trailer park and kept his car in sight until he parked. We turned left and went until we could turn right. That road took us to the back of the trailer part. We turned right twice and that put us on the road that passed his trailer. As we approached his trailer, we checked his car's tag, and it was still the same as the one I had copied down before. We drove out of the trailer park and found a place to pull over so we could figure out what to do next.

Sean spoke up first, "Well, we know he is the shooter now. The problem is that we have no idea how the other two men are connected to the shooting. I think the recording we have would be enough to tie the shooting to him and Sgt. Carson. If we were to arrest this shooter and Sgt. Carson, it would alert the other two men. At this point, we have no concrete evidence on the other two men".

I said, "What if you run the shooter's tag number to see if there are any warrants out for him. If we get lucky and there are warrants, you could arrest him. That would give you a reason to get a search warrant to search his trailer. Who knows what you might find? You might at least we should find the money he was paid for the murder. And based on what he said, he apparently still has the sniper's rifle. If you can just let Sgt. Carson find out about his arrest for the warrants, he may panic and make a mistake".

Samantha chimed in and said, "Even if Sgt. Carson doesn't do anything, it may be time to bring one or both of the other men in for questions. When they find out that the shooter has been arrested, one of them will likely crack, especially if you go ahead and arrest Sgt. Carson. The main thing is that we should not let the shooter leave town. You do need to be able to legally search his trailer before he has time to leave town".

Sean spoke up, "You both are making sense. How about I take both of you into the police department and make you detectives? The two of you are good. The only problem is that Sandton does not have enough crime to support three detectives. In fact, we are so small that I have been surprised that they can even afford one detective.

Seriously, I think you both have made good points. I need to arrest him now so that he does not leave town. Backup officers will also assist me in arresting Sgt. Carson in the morning before the news of the arrest of the shooter is public knowledge. I should then bring in the other two men for questioning.

I am sure Sgt. Carson will lawyer-up. I imagine the other two will also. However, if the questioning stresses that the four of them are going to be charged with murder, the other two men may not want to be lumped in with Sgt. Carson and the shooter. I think this is the best path forward. I will call for a squad car to come assist in the arrest.

I will need you two to stay back since he may not come in without a fight. Take me back to get my car. I will wait until the squad car gets here and we will go back to make the arrest. You two can go home and I will call you when I get back to the station.

I said, "Sean, that is not going to work. He could just decide to get his stuff together and leave while we are getting your car. You stay here and watch his trailer. Samantha and I will go get your car and bring it back here to you. When the squad car gets here then you can go ahead with the arrest. Someone needs to be here in case he tries to leave. I will be glad to stay instead of you if you would like".

Sean said, "You are right, I will stay here and keep watch until the squad car gets here. When you get back with my car, you can go home. That is a good idea. Let me know when you get back so I can get some of my gear out of the trunk".

As we started to leave, I turned and said, "Sean do not to try to be a hero. Wait until the squad car gets here, even if he tries to leave. He can be found later if necessary". Sean smiled but said nothing. I knew what that meant. That is exactly what I would do if I were in his shoes. I would do whatever I had to do to keep him from leaving with all the evidence.

CHAPTER 28

THE UNEXPECTED HAPPENS

Sean got out of the car and started to walk back to the trailer park. Samantha and I got back on the road and headed to the bowling alley. I said I would drive Sean's car back. We found the car where we left it. As we started back to the trailer park, I had an uneasy feeling in my stomach. It was like in Afghanistan when an assignment falls apart for no reason. I called Sean but got no answer. That did not feel right. I called Samantha and told her I could not reach Sean and that I felt something was not right. I asked her to part on the street near the trailer park.

Back at the trailer park, Sean walked back toward the shooter's trailer so he could watch for any signs of him leaving. What he did not know was that the shooter had noticed a car behind him on the way back to the trailer park, which was unusual at 10:00 pm. Normally, no one was out this late in the area. When he saw a car go past his trailer toward the exit, he got suspicious. He got his Glock and the silencer and went out the back door of the trailer. He purposely left a light on in the bedroom. He was almost packed up and figured he would leave tonight anyway.

He crept around a few of the trailers going back towards the front of the trailer park. He had not gone far when he spotted movement about 100 yards ahead, so he stopped and watched. The person was walking down his road, but he was not walking like someone who was going back home. He was walking slowly and appeared to be avoiding the streetlights.

When Sean got 30 to 40 yards from where the shooter was hiding, the hit man who had already killed Father Bishop knew he was going to have to kill again. When he got about 25 yards away, the shooter took aim and shot. He saw the man go down. He watched for a moment and saw no movement. Because he had used a silencer, his shot did not make much sound. He turned and walked back to his trailer. He knew now that he had to pack his things and get out of the area. It only took him 5 minutes to pack, and he got in his car and left the trailer park through a back exit. He got back on the main road and headed away from Sandton, thinking he would go to Florida. He thought Miami would be a good place to spend a couple of days.

The shooter had left just before Preston had arrived at the entrance of the trailer park. Since Preston could not get Murphy on the phone, he parked off the side of the road at the entrance. When Samantha drove up, he told her he was going to look for Sean. He told her to stay in the car and wait for the policeman that Sean had called. She shook her head in agreement and told him to be careful. While she was sitting in the car, she saw a truck pull into the road about a quarter mile ahead going south away from Sandton. She did not pay much attention to the truck, but did think it strange since there was not much traffic out here this late at night.

As Preston walked down the road towards the shooter's trailer, he noticed that practically all the lights in the trailers were off. He tried Sean's phone again but did not get an answer. He thought he heard a faint ringing but was not sure. He walked a little faster. Up ahead about 50 yards, he saw something on the side of the road, but could not make out what it was. It could be a bag of trash, but he had an uneasy feeling. When he got halfway to the object, he realized it was a body.

Afraid it was Sean; Preston ran toward the fallen figure as he called Samantha. In an almost whisper he said, "Call 911. Send them to the trailer. Tell them "Officer Down"!" Then he hung up. He bent over and felt for a pulse on Sean's neck. He heard a groan and quietly told Sean not to move. Sean could not speak, and I looked ahead at the shooter's trailer. There was no truck, and the lights were off. I decided the best thing to do was to stay with Sean until help arrived.

I called Samantha and told her that Sean was alive but hurt. I asked her to wait for the ambulance or the policeman that Sean had called and to bring them back down towards the shooter's trailer. The police car arrived first. Two officers jumped out of their black and white and ran down to where Sean and Preston were. Sean was still lying on the ground, unresponsive. One of the policemen asked me who I was. I told him that Sean and I were together when we got a tip that Father Bishop's shooter was in the area. We had left his car about 5 miles back toward Sandton. About that time the ambulance arrived. The paramedics immediately went to work on Sean. One of the paramedics came over to the policeman and me and said that Sean had been shot but would be okay. I told him to let me know, when he was able to talk. He looked at me and said, "Who are you"?

I said, "I am Preston Bourne. Sean and I were following a suspect in the shooting of the priest in Sandton. I went to get his car and equipment. When I got back, I found him like this".

The paramedic said that they were going to have to leave and take him to the hospital. He did not think he would be able to talk for a few hours. He said that they would be taking him to Sandton General Hospital. I thanked them and told them to take real good care of him.

I turned to the policeman I had been talking to. I said, "Sean can fill you in on the details about how we ended up here. I will be at the police department in the morning". I think my confident attitude and tone of my speech made him a little afraid to pressure me any further about who or what I was.

After the ambulance left, I went over to Samantha. I had already told her about how I found Murphy, so she was up to date. She said that while she was sitting in the truck, she noticed a car pull out on to the road about a quarter of a mile heading away from Sandton. It probably was nothing, but since that was very little traffic on the main road, it just seems a little strange. I thought for a split second and said let's go. We jumped into Samantha's car and took off down the road. Samantha looked puzzled and said, "What are we doing?"

I said, "It is a long shot, but if that was the shooter, he may be driving pretty close to the speed limit. Maybe not, but I am going to see if we can catch up with him". Samantha said, "What will we do if we do catch up with him?"

All I could think to say was, "I haven't figured that out yet". Samantha said, "You know he has about a 10-minute head start on us. I am beginning to wonder about you". I turned toward her and grinned, "Don't you just love a man full of surprises?"

I got our speed up to about 90 miles per hour. That was about as fast as I wanted to drive at night. We kept up that speed for more than 30 minutes. Samantha said, "Look up ahead. I see taillights about a mile away. I have no way of telling if that is him, but it is someone. Preston, I think we are about 25 miles from Burtin South Carolina. We may run into policemen in about 20 miles".

I said, "What I would like to do is to catch up to him and pass him before I slow down. If we can get far enough ahead to be out of sight, we will find a place to pull over and watch for him. Hopefully, as we are passing him, we can see if it is the shooter's truck. Samantha, could you call 911 and ask for the Burtin county sheriff. Tell them it is an emergency".

When Sheriff Thompson got on the phone, Samantha put it on speaker so we both could talk and listen. I said, "Sheriff, I am Preston Bourne from Sandton. Detective Murphy and I were following up on the guy that shot the priest in Sandton last week. We had followed him to his trailer in my car. We realized that Detective Murphy's equipment was in his car a few miles back up the road to Sandton. My wife, Samantha and I went back to get his car and he was going to stand watch on the shooter's trailer. I called Murphy's phone several times but got no answer. When I got back to the trailer park, I quietly went looking for him. I found him on the ground shot. There were no lights on in the shooter's trailer, but I chose not to approach the trailer until the backup that Sean had called arrived. When the backup arrived along with the ambulance, the officers approached the trailer and determined that the shooter was not in the trailer. The ambulance took Sean to the Sandton General Hospital and the officers went with them back to Sandton. I rejoined my wife, Samantha who was in the truck back on the highway. She had seen a truck get back on the highway about a quarter of a mile toward Burtin.

We are not sure if it is the shooter that shot Detective Murphy and the priest in Sandton, but I decided to try to catch up and determine if it is the shooter. What I was wondering, could you set up a roadblock that looked like a wreck so that if he were the shooter, he would just assume that it is a wreck and not start shooting at someone else. I know it is a short notice, but I did not have any other ideas about stopping him without endangering anyone else".

Sheriff Thompson said, "I understand. I have known Detective Murphy for many years. I hope he okay. By the way, call me John. As far as the roadblock, how far are you from Burtin?"

John, I think are about 25 miles from Burtin. I am trying to actually catch up to the shooter and pass him to make certain it is his truck. I am going 90 miles per hour. If I catch up and pass him and it is the shooter's truck, we will get far enough ahead of him to allow me to pull over without being seen. We will wait until he passes and then pull back in behind at a safe distance. Do you think you have enough time to get set up to safely stop him?"

John said, "Yes that will give me enough time to get an

ambulance out to block the road. I will also get a deputy to stop in behind the ambulance to make it appear that other cars are waiting to get past the accident. Will he recognize your car? If not, you can pull in behind him to block him in, but do not get out of your car and put you and your wife in danger. I will try to walk up to his car to explain that there has been a wreck and it will be cleared up in a few minutes".

I reminded the sheriff that he had already killed one person and shot Sean. I said "Please do not take any chances. We know who he is and if he should get away, we can find him later. It is not worth getting some else shot. We will keep this line open so we can update each other. We are approaching his car now. I will be passing him pretty fast, but we should be able to determine if it is his truck".

Samantha spoke up and said "Yes, it is his truck and his tag number. I am going to make certain that he can see that it is a man and a woman in our car so he will not have a reason to suspect we are following him".

John said, "As you get a little closer to Burtin, there will be several curves in the road and a few roads going off to the right. If you are far enough ahead, you will be able to let him pass without being seen. Let me know after he passes you. What type and color is your car?" Samantha said, "It is a black Lexus SUV. The shooter is driving a dark green Ram truck".

John responded, "That is not what I wanted to hear. I will not be able to see his hands to make sure he does not have a gun. I have another idea though. I will try to see if he is willing to help get someone involved in the wreck out of their car. Hopefully, he will agree to get out of his vehicle and help. If he does, I can make certain he does not have a gun. If he will not agree to help, I will have to do something else".

"John, we have one handgun in our car. We will stay out the way, but I know how to use guns, because I was a Marine sniper. We are now approaching a curve, so I am going to slow down and turn on the next road to the right. We will turn around as quickly as we can so we can watch for him".

After 15 seconds I said, "Okay, we are turned around and hidden pretty well. I will turn my lights out completely. It looks like some head lights are coming around the curve". After he passed, Samantha told John that it was him that just passed. I also told John that since we had passed him earlier, we would have to be careful and stay back a good distance so he cannot make out our SUV and get suspicious. John agreed, so now it was a waiting game.

After a couple of miles, another car entered the highway going toward Burtin. This was actually good because it gave us some cover. I passed that along to John so he would know where we were. I told John that we just passed mile marker 174. He said that the roadblock was set up about 5 miles ahead at mile marker 179. All three cars were now driving at the speed limit and were spaced about a quarter of a mile apart. This was perfect since we wanted to not arouse suspicion. We began to approach another large curve and all three cars kept going. We were approaching mile marker 178. Up ahead we could see the flashing lights of the paramedic's vehicle. The sheriff's car was there with its blue lights.

All three cars started slowing down. As the shooter's car

approached wreckage scene, the sheriff came out from behind the paramedic's vehicle and ran up to the shooter's vehicle. The shooter rolled down his window and John began his appeal for help. "Sir, I hate to ask but we need help getting a lady out or her wrecked car. Would you mind helping". There was a moment of hesitation, but the shooter's door began to open.

When he and John started walking toward the supposed wreckage, two deputies stepped out from behind the vehicle with their guns out. The surprised shooter did not have time to respond before John and one of the deputies grabbed him and got him to the ground and handcuffed him. The shooter protested of course, but John read him his rights.

As I walked up to John and the shooter, I told John I was making a positive identification of him as the man who shot the priest. At that point the shooter stopped protesting and said he wanted to speak to his lawyer. John responded that there would be time enough for that later.

I asked John to step aside so I could talk to him for a moment. When we were out of hearing range from the shooter, I said, "John, can you take him to the Burtin jail and hold him there until tomorrow. I would like Samantha and me to get back to Sandton to check on Sean". John said that would not be a problem. He said that he would make sure it was late tomorrow afternoon or evening before they transferred him to Sandton.

I mentioned that I was almost certain that the money he was paid to shoot the priest and the rifle used to do that would be in his truck. John said that he would make certain that the truck was searched and everything in the vehicle would be kept to ensure a chain of custody was maintained.

I told John that if he did not need Samantha and I for anything that we would head back to Sandton to check on Sean. After we got in the car I turned to Samantha and said, "Can I throw a honeymoon or what?" Samantha grinned and said, "You really know how to make a woman feel special. In the future people will ask, "How was your honeymoon". Our real honeymoon will have to be really grand to crowd out the memory of our first honeymoon. You should start planning now". I told her that was already in the works. I hoped she did not ask how far along the planning was, since we had an agreement not to keep any secrets from each other. Luckily, she did not dig any deeper in the honeymoon issue.

As we were driving, I told her that I would like to stop by the hospital to check on Sean, even though it was late and surely after visitation hours. When we arrived at the hospital, we went to the reception desk. The lady on duty informed us that visitation hours were over. I told her we needed to check on Detective Murphy. I explained what had happened to him and that I had found him after he was shot and that we were after the man that had shot Father Bishop. When I said that her facial expression changed immediately. She said that she was Catholic, and it was a terrible shame to shoot a priest.

She then went on to say that if it were left up to her, "We could take Detective Murphy with us tonight". He was being a real pill, demanding one thing after another. She then said that she was not supposed to allow visitors after hours, but since she knew he was still awake, she would not want to interfere with an investigation. She took us to his room and left.

When I looked at Sean, I said, "I hear you are being a real pill. What is your problem? You only have one bullet hole in you. What is all the fussing about?" Sean said, "I see you must not have been present when they handed out sympathy instructions. My main problem is that they will not let me out of here. See what you can do about that! What happened after the guy shot me. I think I must have passed out. Did he get away?"

I said, "I was really worried, when I first found you.. Before the paramedics arrived, you were not responsive. I could tell you were still alive, but I have not been around people with bullet wounds for quite a while. When they arrived though, they said you would be okay.

When I got back to the truck with Samantha, she said she had seen a car re-enter the highway about a quarter of a mile down the highway from the trailer park. Since he was about 10 to 15 minutes ahead of us, I decided to try to catch up to him. I had to drive pretty fast, but after 30 minutes or so, we did see taillights up ahead.

Samantha called the local sheriff and we set up a plan to attempt to stop him without further shooting. Long story short, it worked, and he is in custody in Burtin. Sheriff Thompson is going to keep him in jail and bring him back to Sandton tomorrow late. I wanted to get with you, assuming you were in condition to talk, to figure out our plan for the path forward".

Sean said, "I'll tell you the path forward…"

"Get me out of this" I interrupted.

"Settle down Sean. That will not happen tonight. We will come back early tomorrow morning. We will see about getting you out then. We can begin putting our plans together. Until you are released, you need to settle down and not give the staff any more reasons to be uncooperative with us tomorrow. Try to get some rest. We now have the shooter in custody. Sheriff Thompson is searching his vehicle and will surely find the money he was paid for the shooting, along with the gun he used to shoot you and the rifle he used to shoot Father Bishop. We are getting close to being able to solve this entire issue".

Sean said, "I think you might be right, about this case and about my being a pill". After a moment he continued, "Have you ever thought of being a detective? You and Samantha make a good team".

I said, "You are right, Samantha and I do make a good team, but I think we will leave the detective work to you. See you in the morning. Be good to the staff, especially the lady at the desk. She is on our side, thanks to me"."

Samantha and I returned home, mostly silent on the ride. When we arrived, I suggested we get a hot shower before we have any serious conservation. Samantha nodded in agreement. While she was showering, I had a glass of wine. It was the right thing to do. It helped my brain to process what had happened in the last 18 hours.

After an extreme rush from adrenalin, there is often a letdown. Today though, the adrenalin flow had happened over and over for me and Samantha. Just knowing we had finally had a break in the case and 95% sure that we had identified the shooter and could end up with the evidence to solve the case kept us excited the whole night. Then when the shooter shot Sean and made a break to get away, it looked like it was all going to fall apart. When we actually captured the shooter, the day ended, but it was somewhat of a letdown. The excitement of unofficially chasing a criminal was gone.

When Samantha finished her shower, I got up to take my shower. I said, "I bet you will council your clients to marry an accountant or librarian and avoid someone like me". Samantha just smiled and said she would never give advice that she would not follow. She left to get a glass of wine. I turned and went to take my shower. When I returned, Samantha was asleep on the couch. I thought that was a fitting end to this adrenalin-filled day. I got a blanket and covered her up and had another glass of wine in the recliner.

CHAPTER 29

IT IS TIME TO TIGHTEN THE SCREWS

The next morning, I woke up and saw that Samantha was still asleep. I tiptoed into the kitchen and made a pot of coffee for Samantha. I did not drink coffee, so I got a Pepsi and went out to the front porch. This place was so peaceful with all the large trees, birds singing and almost no traffic noises. In a few minutes, Samantha came out with coffee cup in hand. She sat down next to me and laid her head on my shoulder. This was the first time in my life that particular event had happened to me. I said, "Could we just stay this way all day today? This moment is perfect. I love your house, this area and you".

Samantha quickly said, "This is not my house, it is our house. That is what makes it so perfect. I agree with you, I could just stay out here all day. However, we have a lot to do today, starting with visiting Sean. We have do decide what to do now. Let's get dressed and start the day".

I said, "Not so fast. I have to keep my strength up. I have to have two eggs, sausage and toast to begin my day". We both had our breakfast and headed back to the hospital. When we got to

Sean's floor, we saw the doctor enter Sean's room. Samantha said, "This should be good. Let's go see if we can add support to Sean about getting released".

Sean looked up and saw us come in. He said, "Tell this doctor that I have to get out of here". The doctor looked at us, then back to Sean. He said he thought it would be best for Sean to stay for one more day for observation. I looked at the doctor and said, "How do you think it will look in the local paper when a headline says, "Local police detective fights his way out of the Sandton General Hospital wearing only his hospital gown" ?" The doctor looked back at Sean and slowly shook his head and said okay. He gave the normal advice to not make sudden moves that could start the bleeding again. When Sean got dressed and we were in Samantha's car, I said, "I think the best place for us to go would be to Samantha's from porch. You can have all the lemonade you want, doctor's orders".

When we got settled on the front porch with lemonades in hand, Sean spoke first, "So where we are now is that we have the shooter in custody. We need to call Sheriff Thompson to find out what evidence he found in the shooter's car. Assuming, the money and both his pistol and rifle were in the car, we can go down to Burtin to talk to the shooter. I feel sure he will lawyer up immediately. But we can still talk to him. My guess is that he knows very little other than his dealings with Sgt. Carson. He certainly understands that we have the evidence from his truck that shows his guilt in shooting Father Bishop and me. He will know he is either going away for a long time or going to die in the electric chair or be shot by a firing squad, a new option in SC".

Sean paused and added, once he knows that we know about Sgt. Carson, he will not have anything to bargain with. I think he will be at a dead end. Do either of you see anything I am missing?"

I said, "I basically agree with you, with one exception. The other two conspirators will not have any way of knowing what he may have seen or heard about them. It may help us break them if they were to get the impression that he had spilled his guts about them.

"I seriously doubt that either of them knows anything about who he is or what he may know about them. Saying this, it means that you need to bring the two other conspirators in soon. The main question is what to do about Sgt. Carson. Word will get around about you bringing the shooter in. Sgt. Carson will have to think that the shooter will eventually give him up to you. I think you should bring all three of the conspirators in today. I would think it best to begin questioning William Jameson. He has the most to lose, since he is living in high society, and well respected in the city.

"I definitely think that Sgt. Carson and the shooter will be almost impossible to crack. The only weakness I see in Sgt. Carson is being a cop, he will not want to go to a prison where he has sent convicts to. He would be in danger all day every day. Depending on how he is questioned, he could be tempted to cooperate if he thought he could get a prison where no one would know him".

Sean looked at Samantha and asked if she had any ideas. She shook her head and said that she agreed with all that I had said.

Sean said, "I sure wish I had both of you on my staff. Wait, I have no staff. I am the only detective. Still, you guys would make great detectives. I agree that it is time to bring them all in, at least for questioning. I think it is time to arrest Sgt. Carson. I will get deputies to pick up the other two for questioning. Hopefully, we can get one to break and try to plea for a lesser charge. I will begin questioning William Jameson with the statement that he is facing an indictment for first degree murder".

"When I tell him that we have the shooter in custody and that we have arrested Sgt. Carson on the same charges, I fully expect William Jameson to cooperate and spill his guts. Just like on TV, the first bird to sing gets the prize. If he does not cooperate, I will try the same approach on Jerry Truman.

There is one other thing that we have to keep in mind. Until I actually can get Sgt. Carson arrested, the two of you should stay here inside. Sgt. Carson could think that his way out would be to find you and shoot you so he could claim that he tried to take you into custody, and you drew a gun on him. Even though we have the shooter, he does not know that. I will let you know when we have him in custody, and it will be safe for you to come out. Do you understand and agree?"

Both Samantha and I shook our heads in agreement and said we understood. Sean said he needed to get to the police station to get the things started. Samantha agreed to take him. We had not inquired about where his car was. I guess it will turn up at the station somewhere.

CHAPTER 30

THE ARRESTS

Sean was determined to get things rolling. He first called Sheriff Thompson in Burtin and found out that they had indeed found $ 40,000 in cash, a Glock model 22 40 caliber pistol and a M21 Rock Island Arsenal 7.62 X 51 NATO sniper rifle. There were also some papers in his truck. Sheriff Thompson told Sean, that included in those papers was a picture of Preston Bourne. He was not sure what that meant, but Sean explained that the conspirators who were in on the murder of Father Bishop wanted the shooter to help them find and shoot Preston. They were going to blame the shooting on him because of his past experience as a Marine sniper.

Sean asked Sheriff Thompson if the shooter had requested to talk to an attorney. Thompson said that was the first and only thing the shooter had said. Thompson said they told him that he would have to do that when he got back to Sandton. Sean asked Thompson how long he thought he could keep the shooter. Thompson said that he thought he might have to take him back to Sandton later today, unless he legally charged him for some crime.

Sean told him to just plan on transporting him back to Sandton around 6:00 pm.

Thompson told Sean that he would personally bring the shooter to Sandton, to limit the number of people that would know about the shooter and why he was being held. Sean told Thompson he really appreciated his help and how he had helped Preston and Samantha. Thompson replied that they are quiet a pair. He said that they were all business and seemed to know just what to do to capture the shooter without any trouble. He then asked, "What do they do for a living?"

Sean just responded, "It is a long story that could only be discussed over a couple of beers". When Sean got off the phone, he knew his next move. He had to talk to the Police Chief, Clarence Stone. This had gone on too long without bringing Chief Stone in on the whole situation.

He figured he would get his butt chewed out for letting this go on this long without bringing the Chief in on what had been going on. But he knew that getting to a successful conclusion was the most important thing. He was not able to predict how Chief Stone would react when Sean told him he intended to arrest Sgt. Carson or bring in the other two conspirators, but he knew it was time to find out.

Samantha dropped Sean off at police headquarters. Sean went in and headed upstairs to Chief Stone's office. When he went in, Chief Stone said, "What are you doing here? You were shot yesterday. Shouldn't you be taking a few days off? By the way, what were you doing that caused you to get shot?"

Sean said, "I am glad you are sitting down. I have a long story to tell you. I was following up on a lead concerning the murder of Father Bishop. I am sorry to have kept you in the dark, but part of the probe included one of our own officers. Do you want the long or short version?" Chief Stone thought for a minute, then said, "You had better give me the long version, since it includes one of our officers".

Sean said, "I will try to hit the high points, but if some of this does not make sense, stop me so I can explain. This all started when I got a call from a lady I had met in the past but did not know very well. Her name is Samantha Carter. A few days ago, she called me and asked if I could come over to her house because she wanted me to meet someone. She said that he knew of a potential crime that could be coming up soon. When I got to her house, I met a man named Preston Bourne. He has only been in Sandton for a few months. He was renting a garage apartment from Ms. Carter.

"This Preston Bourne said, he had met a policeman named, Sgt. Carson. They had met a few times in a bar. On the third or fourth time they met Sgt. Carson got interested in the fact that Mr. Bourne had been a Marine sniper.

"He said that Sgt. Carson asked him what he thought about "assisted suicide". It developed into Sgt. Carson asking him to help Father Bishop to basically commit suicide. I will leave out some of the more minor details as to why Father Bishop wanted to commit suicide. We can go into that later.

"The thing is that Samantha and Mr. Bourne did not know what to do. They were afraid that if Preston just turned Sgt. Carson down, he might go ahead with the "assisted suicide" and shift the blame to Mr. Bourne, because of his sniper background. They assumed that with Sgt. Carson's police background he might have been able to make it stick. That is why they got me involved".

Sean continued, "The three of us talked about what could be done, since there was no evidence of a potential future crime. We agreed that we could watch Sgt. Carson's movement and see if anything turned up. Sgt. Carson did meet with two other guys a couple of times and then once met with both guys and Father Bishop. That is when it really got intriguing. There was still no crime.

"Mr. Bourne ordered a couple of GPS trackers and attached them to Sgt. Carson's and William Jameson's cars. Oh, I forgot to mention who the other two guys are. One is William Jameson, the Chairman of the City Council and the other is Jerry Truman, the owner of the Mercedes auto dealership in Sandton".

"Before the murder, Sgt. Carson was still talking to Mr. Bourne about the "assisted suicide". Mr. Bourne decided to put Sgt. Carson to a test. He told him that he had to meet with Father Bishop. Sgt. Carson said he did not think that was a good idea, but Mr. Bourne told Sgt. Carson that Carson had to go to see Father Bishop in person and ask him one more time. Sgt. Carson said he would go talk to Father Bishop later that day.

"Mr. Bourne watched his GPS tracker to see if Sgt. Carson actually went to see Father Bishop. Sgt. Carson called Mr. Bourne that night and said that he had gone to see Father Bishop at his church office and he would not agree to meet Mr. Bourne. Mr. Bourne told me that Sgt. Carson did not go to see Father Bishop at his church office because his GPS tracker had not gone anywhere except to the police station and his apartment.

Mr. Bourne then knew that Sgt. Carson had other plans that he was not sharing with him. From that point forward, Mr. Bourne and Ms. Carter were certain that Mr. Bourne was in danger. They brought me in totally and shared what they knew and what they suspected".

Chief Stone said, "I know William well and have heard of Jerry Truman. I do not understand why you did not come to me at the beginning. I think you should have talked to me, since you were watching William, my boss, and one of your veteran officers, but we will deal with our not bringing me in on what you were doing, later. By the way, what were you doing working with civilians. Continue on".

"I understand, Chief. I am sorry for not coming to you, but things were so circumstantial at the time I did not want to do anything that could damage Sgt. Carson's reputation until I had something more substantial. Up until the very end, we had nothing that could be considered evidence. I even suggested that Mr. Bourne should leave town for a while just in case something did happen so he could prove he was not involved.

"After the murder, things changed rapidly. On Monday, after the Friday shooting, I got a video at the police department that was submitted from an unnamed individual. The person that sent the video said it was a recording of a suspicious meeting between two men that could be connected to the shooting of Father Bishop.

"I reviewed the video and Sgt. Carson recognized Mr. Bourne on the video in the Sandton Steak House sitting at a table by himself. Another man walked up and sat down at the table. He handed a bag to Mr. Bourne who then handed him what appeared to be a thumb drive. The second man then left the restaurant. In a few minutes Mr. Bourne also got up and left.

"Since I now know Mr. Bourne was in the video, I called him and set up a meeting to discuss the video. After watching the video, I have to admit I wondered if Mr. Bourne was involved in the murder and was just using me to establish an alibi. That is when I decided to officially interview Mr. Bourne. I told him to assume that we had not met in the past and answer the questions accurately since others would be listening to his interview.

"When I showed him the video, he admitted that it was him in the video. He said that he had run an ad in one of the local marketplace internet spots. He said the man that came to his table had paid him $300 for the software he was selling, and that the money was in one-dollar bills in a paper bag.

"Mr. Bourne said that when he left the restaurant, he walked down to his bank and deposited the money. He gave me the teller's name who helped him and also gave me the deposit receipt. While this sounded legitimate, I did go to the bank and to verify his story later.

"I told him the interview was over. I told him to watch his GPS tracker on Sgt. Carson's car. I told him that if Sgt. Carson started to go anywhere, he should call me so we both could follow him to see where he was going. I forget if I told you that one time before the murder, Mr. Bourne followed Sgt. Carson using the GPS tracker. He followed Sgt. Carson to an abandoned bowling alley south of town. When Sgt. Carson pulled into the bowling alley parking lot, he went along-side a truck that was there. Mr. Bourne went on past the parking lot and pulled over and got out of his car.

"He got as close to the two vehicles as he could without being spotted. He could not hear anything they were saying, but he did see Sgt. Carson pass something to the man through the lowered windows. Then Sgt. Carson drove off. After he left, the man in the truck left the lot and went south away from Sandton for about 5 miles to a trailer part. All Mr. Bourne knew for sure was the man's truck tag number. It was a Georgia tag registered to Bobby Sanford. There were no arrest warrants out on Bobby Sanford in Georgia so that seemed like a dead end.

"We did not think too much about the man we thought was Bobby Sanford. However, after the murder and Mr. Bourne got back in town, he called me and said that Sgt. Carson's car was on the move again. We agreed to follow him again. I asked which road Sgt. Carson was on. This time it appeared he was going back down south of Sandton.

"We finally met up a couple of miles from the bowling alley parking lot. It turned out that Mr. Bourne and Ms. Carter were in their car together. I followed them to the abandoned bowling alley parking lot. Sure enough, Sgt. Carson pulled into the bowling alley parking lot.

"We went past the parking lot and pulled into the vacant building parking lot next to the abandoned bowling alley. We parked with our cars out of sight. We hurried back to the bushes between the two buildings. Sgt. Carson again passed something through the vehicles' windows. We could not hear everything, but we did hear Sgt. Carson say that he would take care of the other guy and that it would probably be best if he left the area soon.

"Sgt. Carson left the lot first. We walked back to our cars and decided to follow the other man, that we thought was Bobby Sanford. Mr. Bourne said that he thought he knew where Bobby Sanford was going so, we hopped into Samantha's car to follow him. We stayed far enough behind the man's vehicle to make certain he would not think he was being followed. When he turned into the trailer park we pulled over on the side of the highway.

Mr. Bourne said, "He may be leaving soon. What do we do?" I spoke up and said, "I should not have left my car. My gear is in the trunk. How about the two of you go back and get my car, since it only about 5 miles back. I will stay here and watch to make sure he does not leave. If it looks like he is leaving I will call you, then we will decide what to do.

"They left, and I started walking down toward his trailer. I had only gone a short distance and he shot me. When Mr. Bourne got back and found me, I was unconscious. He called for backup and the ambulance. When back officers and the ambulance arrived, they loaded me up, still unconscious and left. Mr. Bourne told the officers that he and I were following the shooter of Father Bishop and that led us to his trailer park. Mr. Bourne told the officers that they would follow them to the hospital to be with me.

"Mr. Bourne told me later that Samantha saw someone entering the highway down the road about a quarter of a mile. They thought it could have been the shooter, so they took off after him. I was unconscious or I would not have let them follow the suspect.

"The bottom line is they called Sheriff Thompson from Burtin, and they asked him to set up a roadblock to capture Bobby Sanford. It was quite ingenious the way Mr. Bourne suggested to get him without any more shooting. It actually worked out perfectly. After Sheriff Thompson had secured Bobby Sanford, he and his officers searched Bobby Sanford's truck. They found a substantial amount of cash in Bobby Sanford's truck, along with the rifle he likely used to shoot Father Bishop and the piston with silencer that he shot me with.

"There is one more item that deals with Sgt. Carson. When Mr. Bourne met with Sgt. Carson, he was offered money to be the shooter. Mr. Bourne was afraid to tell Carson that he would not go through with it, for fear of retribution. He agreed to receive the money. He cleared that with me and said he would then turn it over to me as evidence. I took the money and deposited it in the evidence room. The payoff was actually from a third man but handled through Sgt. Carson. When Sheriff Thompson arrested Bobby Sanford, Mr. Bourne confirmed that this was the man that gave him the money authorized by Sgt. Carson.

"That pretty well catches you up to date. What I want to do now, with your approval, is to arrest Sgt. Carson and bring in William Jameson and Jerry Truman for questioning. We do not have any hard evidence of how much William Jameson and Jerry Truman knew about the murder. I am hoping that when we tell William Jameson and Jerry Truman that we have arrested Father

Bishop's shooter and Sgt. Carson they will realize the trouble they are in.

"We can tell them we have surveillance of them meeting with Sgt. Carson and Father Bishop and later with just Sgt. Carson. We can tell them they will be charged for first degree murder, unless they can show us a reason for a lesser charge. Hopefully, one of them will break and give us a confession that will fill in the missing information.

"Honestly, at this point we do not have any hard evidence against William Jameson, Jerry Truman or Sgt. Carson. Unless Bobby Sanford breaks and gives us some proof that Sgt. Carson paid him to shoot Father Bishop, we cannot prove Sgt. Carson had anything to do with the murder. The fact that he met with Bobby Sanford is circumstantial and is not proof of any wrongdoing. So Chief, will you allow me to go ahead with the plan as I have outlined it to you?"

Chief Stone hesitated for a moment, then said, "I don't like it at all. This could blow up in our face. If it gets out that we are trying to tie William Jameson in on the murder plot without any proof, it will likely cost me my job. Can't you come up with a way to delay bringing the others in for questioning and try to get more evidence? Obviously, we have enough to charge Bobby Sanford with murder. But we have nothing else on the other three.

"Jameson could lawyer up and then fire me for dragging him into this with no evidence. Jerry Truman could also file a lawsuit against the police department and city for damaging his reputation. Let me think about this for a couple of hours and talk to our departmental lawyer to see what he might have to say.

You do know what you have done by not bringing me in on this and you working with two civilians, one of which could also be involved in the crime could cost both you and me our jobs".

I said, "Okay, I will hold off with the other three. I do understand that I probably should have talked to you, but we were not sure who all could have been involved. I was trying to be careful not to do anything to hurt Sgt. Carson's reputation unless we had some real evidence that he was involved with the murder. With your permission, when Bobby Sanford arrives, I will process him in and charge him with first degree murder and attempted murder of me. Let me know what you and the lawyer come up with about Sgt. Carson and the other two men".

It will be hard to deal with Sgt. Carson since we are not going to do anything about him now. After I thought about it for a few minutes, it became clear that I need to draw him into the investigation to see what his reaction. I did not share that we knew of his connection with the shooter, because it might make him think he was a suspect himself.

I walked into Sgt. Carson's office, and he looked up and was startled to see my bandaged arm and upper chest. He said, "What happened to you?" I told him I was in the process of arresting the Father Bishop's shooter and he pulled a gun and shot me. Thank God, he was later captured by Sheriff Thompson from Burtin.

Sgt. Carson said, "Thankfully, he was not a better shot. How did you know he was the shooter? It sounds like you did some real detective work".

I laughed and told him I had a good tip and followed up on it. I then told Sgt. Carson that I had some things to do to get ready for when Bobby Sanford arrived, so I would talk to him later. I did not want to give Carson too much information. I wanted his curiosity to cause him to make a mistake. Up to now, he had been very good at scheming and covering his tracks. The one thing that had worried me was that Carson might still try to find Preston to remove him as a witness to the murder of Father Bishop.

Sean went back to his office and called Preston and told him that Chief Stone did not think they should arrest Sgt. Carson or the other two men without some better evidence.

Chief Stone said, "The truth of the matter is that we do not know why Sgt. Carson and the shooter wanted Father Bishop dead, and we did not know how the other two men fit into this whole situation".

Sean said, "I hate it, but the Chief is right. Without some evidence of why Father Bishop was killed and how all the players fit in the puzzle, we would be setting ourselves up to be sued and fired from our jobs. For now, that means you will need to be careful if you leave Samantha's house. I really think that Sgt. Carson would like to eliminate you. He knows you could shine the light on his involvement in the murder".

Preston said, "Samantha and I will be watching Sgt. Carson's GPS and make sure that we stay far away from him. If we go out to eat, we will go to Brandenburg. Sean, keep us posted on what is going on".

CHAPTER 31

THE WAITING GAME

I told Samantha about my conversation with Sean. She was surprised that the three men were not going to be arrested now. She was immediately worried about my safety. I tried to convince her that I had been through much worse situations while in the Marines, but that did no good.

I changed the subject. I said, "Samantha, we need to talk to your friend Danny. We need to let him know we plan to get married. He said that you were like his little sister. I think you should invite him over so we can talk to him. We don't want him to hear from someone else".

Samantha agreed and said she would call him now to see if he could come over tonight. She got her phone and dialed his number. When he answered, she said, "Danny, I have some things I would like to discuss with you. Could you come over to my place tonight?" Danny said he would be over around 8:00.

When he arrived and came into the den, he spotted me and said, "What are you doing here? I thought Samantha had a few things to discuss with me". Samantha told Danny to have a seat, and she would explain the reason she wanted him to come over. She offered Danny a drink, but he did not want anything. It was apparent that he was uncomfortable with my being in the room.

Samantha began, "Danny, when Preston came over that first day, it was apparent that he was qualified to do the work I needed on this house. I think he told you that he had rented the garage apartment. He started doing some of the handyman work on the house. We naturally talked and got to know each other. To be honest with you, when he first got here, we hit it off with each other. We talked for hours, then days. We both realized that we were becoming more than just two people working together.

"There is a lot more to the story about what has been going on with the murder of Father Bishop. We will tell you one day, but we cannot go into details now. You will just have to trust me. Preston and I came to understand that we were like two puzzles with each puzzle missing one piece. This is the long way of saying that we fell in love. We both have no doubts about what we want. We are planning to get married in two or three months".

I thought it was time for me to speak. I said, "Danny, you said that Samantha was like a younger sister. I respect that and we would like to have your blessing. I know this news comes as a shock to you and it will take time for you to process it. This has to seem sudden to you, but Danny, sometimes there are things that happen and when it happens, you just know it is right. Neither of us are teenagers.

"You know that Samantha has a great education and has built a good business. I think I told you I was in the Marines. I probably did not tell you that I was a sniper in Afghanistan, because I do not normally tell people about that. What else I did not tell you, was that I am a chemical engineer and that I had an engineering business before moving to Sandton. I know what you must be thinking. What I said was that I was looking for handyman work. There are reasons that I was not ready to get back into engineering. With Samantha in my life, I realized that I was ready to get back to doing what I do best in the engineering field. We would really appreciate your blessing on our marriage".

Danny said, "You are right this is quite a shock. Samantha, I have known you for more than half your life. I have never known you jump into things. This looks like you may be moving too fast. Know this, all I want for you is to be happy and safe. I do not want to see you go down a path that ends up with you getting hurt. Preston, I do not know much about you. I want you to know, if I ever think you are not treating Samantha properly, you will have me to deal with".

Samantha spoke up, "Danny, I know that Preston mentioned that he was a Marine and a sniper. What he did not tell you was that before becoming a sniper, he was in force recon in the Marines. I found out that means that he was trained in many ways to use force, whether with his hands or other weapons. I do not think he is a good person to make threats to. As kind and thoughtful as he is, I have seen him in action in things that will come to light in a few days or weeks. But all through the last few weeks, his main concern has been my protection".

Danny spoke up, "What the hell are you talking about? Has he put you in danger? What have you been doing that you had to be protected?"

Samantha said, "Danny, we are going to tell you some things

that must stay between the three of us. Preston overheard some information about the murder of Father Bishop. I introduced him to Detective Murphy because I have known him for a few years. We have been working with Detective Murphy to try to gather information about who is involved and why the murder took place.

"Preston was instrumental in capturing the shooter. In no way did he ever put me in danger. He even suggested he could move out of the apartment if it looked like I might be in danger. I mentioned earlier that we both felt like a puzzle with a missing piece. We finally figured out that what was missing in both of our lives was each other. I have never felt this complete and happy, and I think that Preston feels the same way".

Danny said, "That is quite a story. I do want to hear more of the details about what the two of you have been up to, when you are able to talk about it. I have to say that seeing the looks in both of your eyes, it is hard not to accept what you are saying about your feelings for each other. While this does seem sudden, I kind of get what you are saying about being a puzzle with a missing piece. All of your adult years, it did seem like something was missing. I have never seen you look as happy as you look now. I guess that means that I give you my blessing, for whatever that is worth".

I said, "Danny your blessing means a lot to Samantha and me. That is why we wanted to tell you a few months ahead of our wedding. I could tell that Samantha was dying to tell someone, and we wanted you to be first among her friends. I don't have many friends because as a boss she has kept me busy working on the house and I have not had the occasion to meet many people". We all laughed and decided it was time for a beer.

CHAPTER 32

THE SECOND MEETING WITH CHIEF STONE

Chief Stone called me and asked me to come back to his office. When I arrived, I could tell by the look on his face he was not happy. He said, "Sean, I talked with the lawyer, Thurston Wells. We both feel that there are land mines all around this case. As distasteful as it is, we cannot arrest Sgt. Carson, William Jameson or Jerry Truman. We cannot officially bring them in for questioning. We would be opening ourselves up for deformation lawsuits from all three of them. All we know about them is that they met together and also met with Father Bishop. If they said that Father Bishop had reason to think someone wanted to kill him, the whole world would believe that, and we would be the bad guys.

"At this point, we need to arrest Bobby Sanford and charge him with murder of Father Bishop and attempted murder of you. We can see if he is open for an offer from the district attorney depending on whether he will corporate with us in the investigation. I doubt he will take it, but we can try.

"Thurston, our departmental attorney also said that I could privately talk to William Jameson and tell him that we know about his meetings with Sgt. Carson, Jerry Truman and Father Bishop on several occasions to see if he will volunteer anything. It is very doubtful, but it will plant a seed in his mind because he will not know how much we know. I will try to be convincing that I am trying to help him avoid any connections with the man arrested for the murder of Father Bishop. I do not know Jerry Truman so that private meeting will not work on him.

"Thurston and I both think you should question Sgt. Carson about his meeting with Bobby Sanford. You don't have to tell him how you know about it. It would also be best if you do not mention that you know about his meeting with the other two men. If we are lucky, he will try to set up a meeting with the other two.

Sean thought for a moment then said, "Chief, I agree with some of what you said. I disagree with your talking to William Jameson now. I would like to talk to Sgt. Carson first, then wait for a day or two and see if he will try to set up a meeting with the other two men. If he does, we will know about it because of the GPS tracking devices on Sgt. Carson's and William Jameson's cars. We can track them and see if we can pick up any conversation.

"After a couple of days if no meeting is set up, then you could have your meeting with William Jameson. I do agree with your plan to talk to him and let him know that you hope the investigation does not develop any information that he knew anything about the murder. I think that will put some amount of fear in him and he might make a mistake".

Chief Stone said, "That sounds reasonable. I will hold off talking to William until I hear from you. One thing, are you sure you should keep Mr. Bourne involved? He is a civilian and we would not want to get him hurt".

I said, "He is an ex-Marine, special forces, so he is tough. But he also has good instincts for detective work. We will be careful though. I will let you know, if the three men are on the move and where they are heading".

Just then I got a phone call from downstairs that Sheriff Thompson had arrived with Bobby Sanford. I told Chief Stone about it and we both walked downstairs.

We met Sheriff Thompson at the front desk. The Chief thanked Sheriff Thompson for his help and told him we were in his debt. Sheriff Thompson looked at me and asked how I was doing. I responded that I was okay, no thanks to Mr. Sanford. Bobby did not look up or make any comments. I again thanked Sheriff Thompson and said that I would take Mr. Sanford off his hands. I took him to the booking station. Sheriff Thomson told Chief Stone that he had the evidence from Bobby Sanford's truck in his car. They walked out to get it.

I read Bobby his rights and led him to a holding cell. He said he wanted to talk to a lawyer. I decided to give it one last shot. I told him we would help him with that, but I that I had one question for him. I said, "You know that you are charged with murder of the priest and attempted murder of me. If you want to talk to the district attorney to see if there are any options on the table, I can arrange that". He responded he would wait to talk to his lawyer. I said, "Okay" and I called the jailer and asked him to take Mr. Sanford to his cell.

After I finished with Bobby Sanford, I went back to my office.

I called Preston and let him know what we were going to do. I told him to be watching his GPS trackers to see if the conspirators go on the move later on tonight. Preston said he would be watching for movement of the two cars he had monitors on.

I then called Sgt. Carson and asked him to come down to my office. When he arrived, I said, "Have a seat. Sgt. Carson, I just booked Bobby Sanford for murder of Father Bishop and for attempted murder of me. We have the rifle that he used to shoot Father Bishop and the pistol he shot me with. I have information that you met with Bobby Sanford on two occasions, maybe more. That puts our department in a tough situation. Would you care to explain?"

Sgt. Carson looked surprised then said, "I am not sure where you got your information, but it is obviously bad information. I have no idea who this Bobby Sanford is. Where did you hear such a crazy thing? It sounds like someone is trying to set me up".

I just looked at him for a moment and then said, "It is a pretty creditable source. Are you sure you have never met him?"

He said, "Are you saying I had something to do with the murder of my friend, Father Bishop? I do not know any Bobby Sanford. I will be glad to help you in any way I can, even if it is just to remove any doubt about me being involved. What about the guy, Preston Bourne? You know, the ex-Marine sniper. This sounds like it right down his alley. You said you had talked to him about the video. Are you sure he was not involved with the shooter? Is he still in town? I will be happy to help you find him for more questioning".

I said, "Thanks, but I will be able to handle this investigation.

It is a small town and people notice things. I have some leads about who Bobby Sanford met with and I will be checking that out. If I need your help, I will let you know. Guess I had better get busy. Thanks for coming by".

I called Chief Stone and brought him up to date about my meeting with Sgt. Carson. I reminded him to give me a couple of days to see if he met with the other two men. I told him I would let him know if anything turned up.

CHAPTER 33

QUESTIONING BOBBY SANFORD

I let Sanford's lawyer know that I would like to meet with Bobby and him. The lawyer agreed but warned me not to try to threaten Bobby in any way. I assured him that was not my intention. When the three of us were in one of the interrogation rooms, I asked if they wanted anything to drink. Bobby said he would like a beer. I ignored that and the lawyer asked what we need to talk about, since his client would not have anything to say. I started the conversation with, "Bobby, are you actually from Georgia? The tag on the truck is a Georgia tag". Bobby said he moved around a lot doing construction. Then there was nothing but silence.

"Bobby, you know we found a rifle and a pistol in your truck, along with a large amount of cash. I am pretty sure that the ballistics from the rifle will match the bullet that killed Father Bishop. The ballistics from the pistol will likely match the bullet that I was shot with".

The lawyer said, "Sean, you will have the chance to make your case in the court room. Are you just wanting to practice your speech?"

I said, "No, I just wondered if you client understands what he is facing. I thought he might be wondering if the District Attorney would be making any kind of offer before the trial. There are a few items we could use some help with. What do you think Bobby?"

Bobby laughed, "I am sure there are things you would like to know. But I do not know anything about the things you are charging me with. I just came through this town of yours, stayed for a few weeks and was getting ready to move on. I came up on the roadblock, and you know the rest. I have no idea whose guns those were in my truck. Someone must have put them there to try to shift the blame on me since I am a stranger in town. The money is mine, from some work I have been doing before I came here".

The lawyer stood up and said, "This meeting is over. We have nothing more to say. This was a waste of time. Do not have any meetings with my client without me being present. Have a good day".

As they walked out, I said, "Think about it Bobby. Going to a prison for killing a priest and shooting a police detective, you may meet some interesting people. Some may pat you on the back for shooting a policeman, but killing a priest may get you a slap on the back with a shive". The lawyer started to say something, but just stormed out. He told Bobby not to talk to anyone under any circumstances.

I was really proud of myself. I was sitting there talking to the man who shot me, and I did not climb across the table and strangle him. I will never forget the smirk he had on his face the whole time. I suspect the smirk will fade away when he gets in the court room. The judge and jury will see him as the man who killed the local priest and shot one of the city policemen.

After my heart rate settled down, I called Preston to let him and Samantha know about the afternoon's happenings. I reiterated that Sgt. Carson would not be arrested. I told him that Chief Stone would be waiting to talk to William Jameson until we had given Sgt. Carson time to contact and meet with the other two men. I reminded him to be sure to monitor the GPS tracking unit. After my talk with Sgt. Carson, I felt sure he would have to talk to them to let them know about the shooter being arrested. Since neither William Jameson nor Jerry Truman were likely to have been involved in this type of affair, they will have to be terrified. Sgt. Carson would probably have to try to keep them calm.

CHAPTER 34

WAITING AGAIN

After talking to Sean, Samantha and I decided that a glass of lemonade on the front porch was the only thing that made sense. The sun set was going to be a beautiful site, what little we could see through the trees. Our imagination would have to fill the gaps.

I began to think of all that had happened in the last three months since I had moved to Sandton. Somehow, I thought I had left death in Afghanistan only to find that it seemed to be following me. I realized I was thinking out loud.

Samantha spoke up, "Preston, life comes to us in many ways, some which we do not choose. Our challenge is to deal with what comes to us. Along with those challenges, we often get many good things we had not counted on. Our meeting is one of those good things. Actually, a great thing. You did not bring death to Sandton. Sgt. Carson and the other men did. Your being here is how it got solved. When we get old together, and we will, we will look back over what we went through with wonder, amazement and thankfulness. We both have reasons to focus on the future.

The past is with us, and we will not forget it, but we cannot let it control us or rob us of the happiness we need and deserve".

When I looked at her, I realized I had tears in my eyes. I started to speak, but instead I just hugged her. We clinked our lemonade glasses. While we were smiling at each other, the phone GPS app alarmed. Sgt. Carson's car was on the move. He was leaving from his apartment.

I called Sean and told him that Sgt. Carson's car was moving and heading north, presumably toward Brandenburg. Samantha and I will be heading north as fast as we can. Sean agreed to head that way and we kept our phone connection.

As Samantha and I got to the north side of Sandton, the GPS app alarmed again. This time it was William Jameson's car beginning to move. I told Sean, "It looks like we are on".

Sean said, "I wish we knew where they were going and had time to set up some recording devices. We need to get some real evidence".

I agreed and said, "We have to do something else this time. The times before with the three of them was good circumstantial evidence, but nothing that will convict them. This time we do not know if they will be in a restaurant or a motel room. I know both of you are not going to like this, but I have a plan.

"If they are in a restaurant, I will give them a couple of minutes to talk. I will then walk up to their table and get close by Sgt. Carson so he cannot get his gun out. Remember I have been trained for this type of encounter. I am going to make sure the other two men know what they are in for - 1st degree murder charges. After this, Sean you can come up to the table and escort me out as though you want to question me further. They will not know how much I know. Hopefully, one or both of the men will turn on Sgt. Carson sooner or later and cooperate with you. At this point I do not know anything else to try. We cannot get any recordings of their conversations.

"The one part of the plan I have not worked out is what to do if they are not in a restaurant. In a motel room, when Sgt. Carson sees me, he could pull his gun before I could get close enough to disarm him".

Samantha spoke first, "I don't like you putting yourself in that kind of danger. If we just let the law take its course, it could end up with the three of them not being held accountable, but you would still be alive".

Sean spoke next, "I agree with what Samantha said, but if they are in restaurant, I think the risk will be minimized. I agree that putting the fear in the other two might produce results. I do not think it will hurt our investigation in any way. People like them who have not had dealings with crime and law enforcement might panic and either make a mistake or cause them to decide to come forward with information.

"Let's talk about the second possibility. If they are meeting in a motel room, maybe I could knock on the door. When Sgt. Carson lets me in I could use the excuse that I was following Preston Bourne and I thought he may be in the room with you, Sgt. Carson. Then, Preston, you come in the door and make your speech to the group. Then like in the restaurant version, I could take you out before anything happens. This would also leave them to wonder what you know and what I may do with the information.

Preston looked at Samantha and said, "I understand your concern and I will not take any risks that I think goes beyond my ability to handle. The problem with doing nothing is that as long as Sgt. Carson is not under arrest, he could still look me up and shoot me and claim that it was in self-defense. As long as he is free, he can bring up that I am an ex-sniper and that I was likely involved with Bobby Sanford. With me dead and him a 35-year policeman, it would probably be accepted. What do you think Sean?"

Sean replied, "I hate to admit it, but I think you are right. I think you will have to be looking over your shoulder unless we can prove that Sgt. Carson was the one involved with Bobby Sanford. The other two men are still a puzzle. I am not sure what their involvement was. They are both successful businessmen. It is hard to believe they would be involved in murder, especially in the murder of a local priest. At this point Preston, I think your plan will work with limited risks. I hope they decide to meet in a restaurant, but, if it were me I would not meet in a public place.

Samantha said that Sgt. Carson's car was approaching the Brandenburg city limits and that we will know shortly where they are going. I said that it appears that William Jameson is also approaching the city limits. We are about 2 miles behind at mile marker 182. I then asked, "Where are you Sean?

He responded, "I am just passing mile marker 184, so I am two miles behind you. Just let me know if I need to turn".

CHAPTER 35

THE DAY OF RECKONING

I was driving and Samantha was watching the phone GPS tracking app. She said, "It looks like they are stopping at the Pizza Hut. By the time we get there they should be inside, so we can park without worrying about being seen.

Sean said, "Preston, when you go in, wait at the door until you can determine where they are sitting. I will join you at the door before you approach the table. When I hear you say that all three of you guys are facing 1st degree murder charges, I will come over to the table. Just make sure you can approach behind Sgt. Carson so that he does not see you until you are at the table. Use all your special forces training to keep Sgt. Carson from getting his pistol or taser".

Preston replied, "Samantha, I hate to say it but please stay in the car. I promised Danny I would not put you in danger, and I want to fulfill my promise to you and him. Only Sean and I should go into the Pizza Hut for around a minute. When we leave the restaurant, all three of us will wait in your car to see how long the men stay in the restaurant. I suspect it will be a short wait.

Sean and I approached the Pizza Hut front door. We could see the tables from the doorway. Fortunately, the conspirators were in the far back corner and Sgt. Carson was sitting with his back toward us. I said, "Are you ready, Sean?" I went inside the door and walked around to the wall away from the service counter. I was able to get to the table without any of the men noticing me until I was up beside Sgt. Carson. When he looked up, it totally surprised him. He said, "What are you doing here?"

I said, "I just happened to be in Brandenburg. When I saw you, I wanted to let you and your two friends know that all three of you are about to go down for 1st degree murder".

Before they could say anything, Sean came running up and said, Mr. Bourne, I have been following you and need to ask you some more questions. He looked over at Sgt. Carson, as though he had just seen him, and said, "What are you doing here?" Sgt. Carson fought back his astonishment and said that he was just having dinner with some friends. Sean faced the three men and said, sorry to bother you.

He turned to me and said, "Mr. Bourne you need to come with me. I have a bunch of questions for you". I asked if I was under arrest and he responded, no I just have some follow-up questions for you. We turned and left. When we got to the door, I turned and looked at the three men. I did the old two fingers to my eyes and then to them and smiled.

We went back to Samantha's car. It did not take but a couple of minutes for the three men to come out the front door. From just watching, it was clear the conversation was a heated three-way conversation. It ended abruptly with all three men getting in their own cars and leaving.

Sean and I looked at each other. We started laughing and Sean said, "I was watching them from a distance and when you said 1st degree murder, I hope you saw the look on the two guys faces. It was pure fear in their eyes. I think now is the time for Chief Stone to call William Jameson for a little chat. I now think he should also call Jerry Truman in for a chat. I will have to talk to him about Jerry. I am not sure who would be more effective talking to him. Preston, I think this was a great idea to get them off dead center. I think one of them will see the handwriting on the wall or at least make a mistake that will tie them into the whole murder plot. Are you sure you would not like to become a detective?"

I looked at him and then at Samantha and replied, "I am sorry, I only work with Samantha. We are a team. It is all or nothing". Sean left to get into his car. We started our car and left for home.

I gave Samantha a complete explanation of what had happened inside the restaurant. I could tell she was excited. I told her that I thought it had gone as well as it possibly could and that now we needed to wait and see how the meeting between Chief Stone and William Jameson goes.

Samantha asked, "Did the appearance of Sean come off as a natural happening or did it appear staged?" I replied, "It seemed natural. Sgt. Carson looked truly surprised and the other two did look a little terrified. When we started to leave, the men did not say anything or do anything. If I am being honest, it actually felt good. It was like an assignment that went just as planned. The only question is, can we get one of the two men to break and tell us how they are involved in this affair.?"

Samantha was quiet for a few minutes. She then said, "Preston, I have to admit. Even though I believe you are well qualified in your military training, my heart was racing while you were inside the Pizza Hut. It did not settle down until you were back in the car. I really cannot stand the thought of losing you".

I said, "I appreciate and understand that. I meant what I told Danny. I will not do anything that puts you in danger and that also means that I will be careful about myself, because I am your protector for life. I wouldn't have it any other way". She held my free hand all the way home.

When we got home, I said, "I hope Danny is not hiding in the woods to make certain that I am staying in the apartment. Two or three months is a long time to wait for our public wedding. What if we moved that date up? Neither of us has family that have to travel here".

Samantha said, "I agree with the idea, except that I want the trial over and done with. When we have the wedding, and don't forget the honeymoon, I don't want either of us thinking about the trial of Sgt. Carson".

I said, "I agree. "Lets' go to bed Mrs. Bourne".

CHAPTER 36

THE MEETING WITH WILLIAM JAMESON

The next morning, Sean called Chief Stone as soon as he got in. Sean said, "I would like to come up to your office to explain the events of last night". Chief Stone said to come on up. When they got seated, Sean began, "The GPS tracking units on both Sgt. Carson's and William Jameson's cars alerted that they were on the move. Preston called me and said that they were heading north toward Brandenburg. Preston and Samantha were following the GPS tracking system, and I agreed to meet them when the cars indicated that they had reached their destination.

"On the way to Brandenburg, Preston called me and said that he was thinking about what to do when we got to their meeting place. He pointed out that without recording devices their meeting would not be proof of any wrong doings. He said he had a plan that might force William Jameson or Jerry Truman to panic and decide to cooperate with us. His plan was that once the three men got together, he would approach them. He would make sure he was close enough to Sgt. Carson to make sure that he could not pull a gun on him.

"What he did after he got into the restaurant with the men was the best part of his plan. Standing there in front of them, he told the three of them that the shooter had been arrested. He then looked at them and said they would soon be facing 1st degree murder charges. As we had planned earlier, I approached the group and said that I had been following Preston to question him about our previous meeting. I then asked Sgt. Carson what they were doing there. He said he and his friends were just having dinner.

I then turned and told Preston to come with me and we left. As we were approaching the door, Preston turned and looked at the three of them. He used the two-finger thing to indicate that he was watching them. You could almost see the two men squirm. Sgt. Carson just had a grimace on his face. I tell you. Preston is one cool operator. I have developed a new respect for the Marine special forces. I am glad we are on the same side".

Chief Stone said, "Based on that meeting, you still do not know any more than you did before the meeting. So, what is the next move according to the plan?"

Sean said, "This is why we suggested that you wait about talking to William Jameson. Mr. Bourne and I think he is now primed with fear. When you call him saying that you have heard about some meetings in Brandenburg, tell him that you are concerned, and you wanted to make sure that everything is okay. He is surely going to think that you know more than you are telling him. You can tell him that you knew about his meeting with Sgt. Carson, Jerry Truman and Father Bishop. You can just say that it seemed strange that he met with the man that later got murdered and you were concerned. Then wait for his response. If that does not jar him into saying something helpful, you can drop the bombshell. Tell him that you are aware of Sgt. Carson meeting with the shooter a few days ago. That will likely be news to him. Again, at this point if he doesn't break, I would just end the conversation with the statement that the investigation was ongoing, and his meetings would surely come up. Your final statement could that you can't believe that he would be involved with murder.

"If he does not come forward with a reasonable response, I would suggest the same type of conversation with Jerry Truman. That may be better for me to handle, since you do not know him personally. Also, since he was at the table last night, it would seem reasonable for me to follow-up with a few questions for him".

Chief Stone said, "I agree about Jerry Truman. I will make a call to William Jameson now to see if I can go upstairs to his office. I will let you know what he says. If I were you, I would go ahead and call Jerry Truman and see if you could drop by his office this morning. I do not think it would be good to have him come in here. Hopefully, one of these avenues will work out. We are about out of ideas".

Chief Stone called William Jameson to see if he could go up to his office. William said he was awfully busy this morning. Chief Stone said that it was important, and it would not take but a few minutes. William told him to come on up. When Chief Stone got to William's office, he noticed that William looked nervous. He sat down and began, "I know this murder thing has the city in a lot of turmoil. We are trying to get it behind us, and we have made some good progress. I do not know if you have heard that we have arrested the shooter of Father Bishop and Detective Murphy".

William interrupted and said, "He also shot Detective Murphy?" Chief Stone said, "Yes, Sean was following up on a lead and went to the shooter's trailer park. The shooter came out of nowhere and shot him. There was another man working with Sean, who found him shot and called for help. He also found out that the shooter had left the trailer park. He was an ex-Marine. He chased him down, called the Sheriff in Burtin and they captured the shooter without any further shooting.

"The reason I wanted to talk to you is that Sean has information that you had several meetings with Sgt. Carson, Jerry Truman and Father Bishop. I was concerned that you may have gotten mixed up with something without knowing about it. In a case involving murdering of a priest and attempted murder of a police detective, there will be a lot of questions. I just wanted to see if there is anything that you can share with me that might help me head off some of the trouble that will likely come up since you have met with Father Bishop just before he was murdered".

William seemed to be thinking, then said, "I did meet with Father Bishop to discuss the new school that he was planning to start. He thought the city would want to know about it and maybe have a press release. I think I only had that one meeting. Is that any help?"

Chief Stone said, "it does help. There is one thing else though that will be coming out. Sgt. Carson had a couple of meetings with the shooter, before and after the shooting. I am afraid that when it comes out that you also met with Sgt. Carson during that time on more than one occasion, there will be a lot of pressure to explain your involvement. Like I said, when it became a murder of a priest and the attempted murder of a police detective, it becomes a very public investigation. Are you sure that there isn't more you can share with me? I can only help you, if I know what I am dealing with".

William sat silently for a time just staring out the window. His wife and daughter, both of whom he loved dearly, were in his thoughts. Then he looked directly at the Chief and said, "Chief Stone, I would like to talk to you, but first I think I should consult with my lawyer. I may be in trouble, but it would be wise to talk to him first. I will get back to you.

Chief Stone said, "William, we have known each other for several years. I understand that you want to talk to your lawyer. I only suggest you do it soon. If this case progresses to the point of formal charges, it will be for very serious crimes. After that happens, your bargaining power will be diminished. Also, if Jerry Truman comes forward before you, there may be nothing of value you can add. I am not sure if I am making myself clear, but I will tell you that Detective Murphy is talking with Jerry this morning. I have no idea how that will turn out, but if he knows more than you and decides to cooperate you may not have any bargaining power. I am not trying to pressure you. I just do not see you as the type of person to be involved in murder".

William said, "I will talk to Simon Kilgore, my lawyer and get back to you in a few minutes. You are right. I am not the type to get involved in murder. I have some problems right now, but I am not guilty of murder".

Chief Stone interrupted William and said, "When you talk to Simon, be sure to tell him that you have been observed meeting with Father Bishop shortly before he was shot. You have had several meetings with a person who had two meetings with the man that killed Father Bishop and shot Detective Murphy. He needs to understand how serious this is about to become".

Chief Stone got up and left William's office. He went back to his office and placed a call to Sean. Sean did not answer his phone and was likely still talking to Jerry Truman.

Chief Stone looked out his window and saw that William was walking to his car, presumably to go to the lawyer's office. Chief Stone's phone rang. Sean was on the line and told him that Jerry Truman wanted to come down to the station to talk, since his dealership was not very private. Sean said he would be back to the station in about 30 minutes.

Chief Stone decided to call William's cell phone to let him know that Jerry was coming to the station. He suggested that it might be a good idea for William and Simon to come to the station encase he wanted to make a statement. William said that he would call back as soon as he talked to the lawyer for a few minutes.

This whole affair was bothering Chief Stone. He had known William for a long time and considered him a friend as well as his boss. He could not imagine William being involved in murder. He has a nice family, a good job and a good reputation in the city. He had a feeling that all three of these things were about to come under a lot of pressure.

It turned out that William and Simon arrived at the police station about the same time as Sean and Jerry Truman. They both entered the lobby. There was a look of surprise on both William's and Jerry's faces. Before they could speak to each other, Sean took

Jerry to his office and Chief Stone came down to the lobby and suggested that William and Simon go up to his office. When they got to Chief Stone's office, the Chief excused himself and said he would be right back. He walked downstairs to Sean's office and knocked on his door. He asked Sean to come out to speak to him for a moment.

When Sean met Chief Stone in the hallway, he said, "Okay, Chief, how do you want to handle this. So far Jerry had not said anything".

Chief Stone told Sean that William wanted to talk but wanted to talk to his lawyer. He added, "Since you were bringing Jerry to the station, I suggested he come back to the station with his lawyer".

I think we need to get whatever statement they want to make and then you and I can get back together. I basically told William that the first one to cooperate with us would be in the best bargaining position". Sean said that he agreed and would call when he got a substantial statement.

Chief Stone went back to his office and apologized for the delay. When he sat down, he asked Simon what William had told him. Simon said they had not had much time to talk. He said, "How about you bring me up to date with what is going on and how it applies to William".

Chief Stone said, "I will hit the highlights and you can ask questions as you need. As you are undoubtably aware Father Bishop was murdered recently and Detective Murphy was shot. The man that did both shootings has been captured. It turned out that someone met with the shooter on two occasions. William had met with that person on several occasions in addition to meeting with Father Bishop a few days before he was shot".

Simon spoke up, "Am I missing something? Is there a crime in those meetings? If not, why are you trying to bring William into all this?" Chief Stone turned to William and said, "William is this the conversation that you are wanting to have? I called you as a favor and I will not be lectured, as if, I am the one facing potential problems. You need to explain to Simon that the way things are progressing, you could be facing charges of accessory to murder and shooting a police officer. If you have no plans of cooperating with the investigation, then you and Simon can leave for now. I will give you a few minutes to talk it over". Chief Stone got up to leave, but William said, "Please Chief Stone, give me five minutes with Simon, then come back. I want to cooperate with you".

Chief Stone said, "Okay, I will be back". He left the office and went down to Sean's office. He opened the door and went in and sat down. He said, "How are things going here?" Sean said, "Mr. Truman says that he will need to think about what I have told him and talk to his lawyer". Sean turned to Jerry and asked if that was correct. Jerry said, "I am not sure what it is that you want from me. I know about the priest getting murdered, but I didn't kill anyone. I am not sure why you think I would know anything about that".

Chief Stone turned to Sean and said, "Did you explain that we know that someone talked to the shooter on two occasions. We know that Mr. Truman had met with that person on several occasions and also with Father Bishop a few days before he was shot. What we are talking about Mr. Truman are charges for accessory to 1st degree murder and attempted murder of a policeman. What we find strange is that you being a successful businessman being involved in the murder of a priest and attempted murder of a policeman".

Jerry spoke up excitedly, "Wait a minute I have not killed anyone. I think I need to call my lawyer". Sean spoke up, "Jerry, we are not accusing you of anything, yet. I invited you down here to talk. I wanted to hear what you had to say, because it does not make sense that you would be involved in murder. However, as things are falling into place, we know of your meetings with Sgt. Carson, William Jameson and Father Bishop.

We honestly do not understand the three of you being involved with murder, so we are giving you an opportunity to cooperate with the investigation. Obviously, whoever cooperates with us first has the best chance of avoiding the serious charges that will be coming. You have asked for a lawyer and that is your right. Whether you choose to go down with the Titanic is up to you. You are free to go. If we do not hear from you, we will assume you have made your decision. By the way, I have to ask you to not leave town. I will show you out. I will join you upstairs Chief.

When Chief Stone returned to his office, the lawyer was the first to speak. He said, "William is ready to cooperate with the investigation if you can grant him immunity from charges associated with this case". The Chief looked at William and said, "William, you know I cannot do that. We are talking about murder in the 1st degree. You cannot just say that you were involved in that but will cooperate with us if we drop the charges. That is not going to happen"!

William spoke up, "Chief, that is not what I mean. There was something else going on. That was what all the meetings were about. We need to get with the district attorney and come to an agreement. At this point, I know that the path forward is not going to be pleasant, but I knew nothing about the murder. When we meet with the district attorney, we will lay everything on the table. I will not hold anything back".

Chief Stone said, "I will set up a meeting for later this afternoon. In the meantime, do not mention this to anyone or there will be no deal. I will let you know when I can get it set up".

After William and Simon left, Chief Stone called Sean and asked him to come up to his office. Sean sat down in Chief Stone's office and asked how things went with William. Chief Stone said, "It looks like William is going to cooperate. He says that something else was going on that had nothing to do with the murder. I am setting up a meeting with the district attorney, and I think William wants immunity to the murder charges but will detail the other thing that was going on. He thinks his information will show the connection of the two things. We will have to wait and see. What about Jerry? Where do we stand with him? I am getting a sense that the other thing that William referred to was what the connection between the four men was all about.

Sean replied, "I think the two of us need to get Sgt. Carson up here and see what his story is. Let me call him, and we can take care of that now". When Sean called Sgt. Carson's office, he did not get an answer. He then called the front desk to inquire about the whereabouts of Sgt. Carson. The front desk said that he had left a couple of hours ago. They did not know when he would return. Sean turned to the Chief and said, "That is not good. Should I go look for him?"

Chief Stone said, "Yes, I think so. Tell him something has come up that we need his help with. I think it is essential that we talk to him before the district attorney gets here. I sense where this is going, and I want to hear his side before we start talking about deals with the district attorney".

Sean tried calling Sgt. Carson's cell phone, no answer. He then went by Carson's apartment but did not get an answer at his door. His car was not out front. This was beginning to not look good for Sgt. Carson. He called Preston and told him what was happening. He said, " I have not been able to find Sgt. Carson and that I thought that he must know what is going on". Sean reminded Preston to stay put and to be on the lookout for Sgt. Carson. Then Sean thought about the GPS tracking device. Sean asked Preston if Sgt. Carson's car was on the move. Preston checked and said that it was stationary at his apartment. Sean told him that he was at the apartment, but his car was not there. That could only mean one thing. He found the GPS device. He told Preston that He would put out an all-points-bulletin for Sgt. Carson.

Sean said, "Preston, we do not know how dangerous he may be. You and Samantha be on the alert. Don't get separated and have a weapon handy just in case. I will keep you posted".

CHAPTER 37

THE MEETING WITH THE DISTRICT ATTORNEY

This was to be a large meeting. Chief Stone, Sean Murphy, William Jameson, Simon Kilgore and Jennifer Bloom, the district attorney, were all present. Ms. Bloom introduced herself and said, "Mr. Jameson, this meeting will be recorded. Do you understand that the recording can be used against you if there are any subsequent proceedings? Are you here of your own accord?" William said he understood and was here willingly.

Ms. Bloom said, "For the record, those attending this meeting are Police Chief Clarence Stone, Detective Sean Murphy, William Jameson and Simon Kilgore, Mr. Jameson's attorney, and myself, Jennifer Bloom.

Chief Stone started the meeting. He said, "I think we all know why we are here. William Jameson plans to make a statement concerning his involvement with certain individuals. William, I will turn the meeting over to you".

Before William could speak, Simon his attorney spoke up, "Before William gives his narrative, I would like to point out that he is here cooperating with the police investigation of his own volition. He will be admitting to some wrong doings, and we hope his cooperation will be taken into account on his behalf".

William spoke up, "Thanks Simon. I guess the only place to start is from the beginning. There is no good way to say this, so I will just jump in the deep end. I do not remember exactly how it started, but Sgt. Carson, Jerry Truman, Father Bishop and myself got together and were talking about retirement. We all said that we did not have the means for the type of retirement we had always planned on. The other three men were Sgt. Carson, Jerry Truman and Father Bishop.

"Someone suggested that we could skim a little of money off different budgets and stockpile the money. We figured over time we could come up with enough money to supplement our retirement. As it turned out, Father Bishop took some money from the church, and I took some money from the city council project funds. Jerry Truman had a way to run the money through his car dealership to a private fund. Sgt. Carson was there to listen for any hints of money missing from the city or church funds and figure out how to deal with it if it came up.

"Our 'retirement funding' has been going on for about four years. The 'retirement' account grew to approximately four million. We met occasionally to discuss things. In one of our meetings, Father Bishop said that two guys from his church had suggested that the church use some of its money to start a boarding school. This of course panicked Father Bishop. He insisted that we had to return the money to the church. That did not sit well with the group. Sgt. Carson said that he would come up with a plan and present it to the group. He told Father Bishop to give him a few days to develop his plan.

"Sgt. Carson called Jerry and me and set up a meeting with just us. He said that we should tell Father Bishop that we were going to return some of the money but keep out enough to let him retire and move to South America. That was what Father Bishop had said he would like to do. We figured that would settle things down.

"We called another meeting with Father Bishop and told him of our plan. He seemed reluctant at first, but Sgt. Carson talked to him and convinced him to do that and to move to South America and open a bar. Father Bishop had other plans, but Sgt. Carson told him that starting a clinic would raise questions about where he got the money. He suggested that Father Bishop not mention that he was a priest.

"Father Bishop began to like the idea and thought it would work out. He talked to the two men at church, and they formed a committee to develop the plan for the school. I think that Sgt. Carson told Father Bishop that of the approximately two million he had taken from the church account, he would hold out about $300,000 for Father Bishop's retirement to South America. It took some persuasion, but Father Bishop finally agreed.

"After Father Bishop left the meeting, the three of us started talking. Someone said that we had spent a lot of time and effort into building up the retirement fund. They asked why do we have to give all the church money back? The discussion went on that if we did not put all the church money back in their account, they would not have enough money to build the school. We debated on how much money we had to return to the church in order not to raise suspicion.

Jerry said, "What if Father Bishop started having second thoughts or a guilty conscience. If he let it slip out that he was a priest from Sandton, someone here may find out he started the business in South America and wonder where he got the money.

"This discussion showed that there some holes in Sgt. Carson's plan. Sgt. Carson said that he would take care of refining the plan and that we should not worry. That was the last we heard for several weeks. When we got back together, Sgt. Carson had worked out the plan with Father Bishop. He said that he had talked through the need for complete silence in South America about who he was and what he had been before. He said that Father Bishop was very excited about his retirement, so he felt that Father Bishop would be okay.

"Jerry and I were not so sure about Sgt. Carson's confidence, but he said he was taking care of it. That was the last time we met or discussed it. We did hear when Father Bishop made the announcement about starting the school. Jerry and I talked one day, and we agreed that it looked like Sgt. Carson had worked out the details.

William said, "When we heard about the murder of Father Bishop, I called Jerry and we got together. We both had the same question. Could Sgt. Carson have been involved in the murder? We thought that he would not have gone that far. I decided to call him to see what his response would be. When I called, he said that he was keeping an eye on the investigation and that everything was okay. He said that based on what happened, we should not do anything with the money because it could raise suspicion. I asked him directly, "Did you have anything to do with the shooting?"

"He just said, "Are you crazy. I am a policeman". I have to admit, he was not convincing. I called Jerry and told him about the conversation. We both had our doubts but did not think there was anything we could do. That brings us to where we are today. I know my taking money from the city treasury was wrong and there is no justification. The one thing I must emphasize is that Jerry and I did not have any knowledge or suspicion that Sgt. Carson would go as far as murder. Neither of us are innocent in this matter, but we are surely not guilty of murder. We would never have gone along with this if we had known or suspected Sgt. Carson was capable of planning this".

Ms. Bloom asked, "Did you ever hear anything about the shooter or meet with him? I think his name is Mr. Sanford". William said, "Absolutely not. There was never any discussion about anyone else being involved. If Sgt. Carson had mentioned bringing in anyone else, we would not have agreed to anything except giving the church money back".

Jennifer said, "Who has control of the money taken from the church and city?" William said, "Jerry Truman has handled depositing the money in a bank in Brandenburg. It was put in an account set up for the four of us. I am not sure whose name is on the account".

Jennifer said, "I think that should be about all we need to do now. William, I appreciate your honesty and help in understanding what transpired and ended in the murder of Father Bishop and attempted the murder of Detective Murphy. To be honest with you, there will be charges coming for the fraudulent handling of the city's money. But I do believe that you were not involved in the murder. We will be in touch with you, Mr. Kilgore, about what we do from here.

Jennifer said, "William, I do not think you are a flight risk. I am not going to ask for bail. Just stay around so we can put this behind us". William said, "I want to thank you all. You could have taken a much different way to handle this. I am truly sorry this all happened, but I appreciate what all of you have done".

This ended the formal meeting of the group. William Jameson, Simon Kilgore and Jennifer Bloom stood and left Chief Stone's office. After the meeting broke up, the Chief asked me to stay behind for a few minutes. He said, "Bring in Jerry immediately. If he wants, he can bring in his lawyer with him. Also, check on the progress in locating Sgt. Carson. Ask Jennifer to get you a search warrant for Carson's apartment. You know, that is the first time that I have not referred to him as Sargent. He does not deserve the title".

Sean spoke up, "I have been trying to find Sgt. Carson. I have put out an APB for him. I am sure he will turn up. I will bring Jerry in. I talked to him this morning, but he wanted to talk to his lawyer. I will let you know when he is ready to talk to us. If he refused to talk to us, I will arrest him.

I immediately called Jennifer from my office about the search warrant. She said it would be ready when I could get to her office. She said this is a dreadful mess. I do not envy your job.

I said, "Neither do I. Solving crimes is what I do and enjoy. But when it one of our own, it hurts deep down. Thanks for your help on such a short notice".

I picked up the arrest warrant but decided to pick up Jerry first. I called him and told him we needed to talk to him at the police station. He said that it was not a good time. I said, "Jerry, you can come in and bring your lawyer, or I can come get you now. Your choice. This is not a request". He said he would be at the police station in 30 minutes and would try to have his lawyer with him.

I decided that I would use the next 30 minutes to check out Sgt. Carson's apartment. On the drive to his apartment, I called Preston and Samantha. I told them all that had transpired so far today. I mentioned the arrest warrant for Sgt. Carson and that we were about to talk to Jerry Truman. I reminded them to not go anywhere until we knew the whereabouts of Sgt. Carson. Preston said, "You know, I think you have mentioned that a few times. We will be careful".

Sean said, "I know. I don't mean to treat you like a kid; I am just ready for this to be over with no one else getting hurt".

Samantha and I both said, "Good luck with Jerry. Let us know how things turn out with him. Keep us posted on the progress with Sgt. Carson".

Sean went by Sgt. Carson's apartment. He knocked, but no answer. He said, what the heck, and kicked the door in. He smiled and thought, I haven't done that in years. It hurt more than I remember. It looked like Carson had left hurriedly. Some of his clothes were gone. He did not see anything incriminating laying around, so he decided to go back to the office to talk to Jerry. He pulled the door to, as well, as he could. He would send a team back to check out the apartment later.

He arrived back at the station before Jerry and his lawyer. He checked with the front desk to see if there was any word on Sgt. Carson. Nothing yet.

Jerry and his lawyer came in the next few minutes. His lawyer spoke up without any greeting, and said, "What is this all about?" My first impression of his lawyer was that he most likely made a living defending pimps. I said, "I imagine Jerry has told you, so don't play games with me. I am in a good mood, and I don't want you to ruin it. We will go up to Chief Stone's office".

The lawyer jumped in with, "We are not going anywhere until we know what this is all about. Is there a charge against my client?" I turned to Jerry and said, "Where did not find this clown? You want a charge? Right now, murder 1st degree and attempted murder of a police detective is on the table. Is that what you want to hear, or do you want to go upstairs to try for something better?"

Jerry told his lawyer to get lost. The lawyer looked stunned but turned and left. We went up to the Chief's office. I told Jerry, "If you need a lawyer and I think you do; you need to find a better one". In the Chief's office we took our seats.

Chief Stone said, "Jerry this is an informal meeting, but you may want to meet with the district attorney with your lawyer present. As you know, we are in the middle of investigating the murder of Father Bishop and shooting of our Detective Murphy. I know Detective Murphy talked to you this morning. I have reason to believe that you were not involved in the murder, but you do have something that is going to cause you some problems. I am going to be open and blunt with you.

"We have had a meeting with William Jameson, his attorney and the district attorney. William gave us his version of his, your and Sgt. Carson involvement in this whole affair. I am going to offer you the same chance to talk to your lawyer and the district attorney on the record. Since you do not have an attorney present, I am going to tell you that you have a right to have an attorney present".

Jerry stopped him in mid-sentence and said, "That's okay. I know my rights. Call the district attorney and I will call another lawyer. I know this is serious business, and I would like to skip to the bottom line".

We took a recess so I could call Jennifer to see if she could come back to the station. She said, "My, but you are busy. Remind me to not get on your bad side". Sean said, "Who said I had a bad side, I am just a crème puff". She smiled and said she would be right over. Jerry must have a list of lawyers. He made one call and said the lawyer would be over in 20 minutes. I was glad that Sandton was a small town.

When Jennifer and Jerry's lawyer, Gerald Bennett arrived, we went back to Chief Stone's office. After the introductions, Jennifer went through her instructions about the meeting, recording and warning that all that is said will be on record for use later, if required. She said, "I will tell you that we had a similar meeting with William Jameson and his lawyer. He told us about his, your and Sgt. Carson's involvement in what he described as a retirement club. If you get what I am meaning. At this point, I am going to offer you the same thing that I offered him. If your story is the same as his, 1st degree murder will be off the table. If your story is different or you do not cooperate with us, accessory to 1st degree murder and attempted murder of Detective Murphy will still be

241

possible charge. If you would like a few moments with your lawyer, we can give you that". Jerry's lawyer said, "What do you mean by the retirement club". Jerry said, "If we could have 5 minutes, I would like to explain a few things to Gerald".

We left the room and got some water. In a few minutes, Jerry motioned us back in. He told his story, which was almost verbatim with William's. Jennifer said, "Mr. Truman, your story agrees with William's. I will tell you what I told him. I do not see you as a person that would knowingly get involved in a murder. The stealing of the money that was stolen and handled by you is a crime. There will be a penalty, but I will not be going for accessory to murder.

"If this is your statement, Detective Murphy will let you write it out and you will be free to go, as long as you do not leave town. We will get together later to explain the path forward. I will not be asking for bail. I hope you do not disappoint me and do something stupid".

Jerry said, "I can assure you that I will do as you say. I appreciate your taking the time to meet with me. Gerald, do you see any problem with the plan as laid out?" Gerald said, "I think under the circumstances, you are very fortunate. If you need, I will check your written statement. Naturally, I will be with you when you are arraigned in court".

We ended the meeting, shook hands and left. It had been a very productive day. The only disappointment was not finding Sgt. Carson, but that will come.

CHAPTER 38

SGT. CARSON SHOWS UP

Sean called Samantha and I to tell us the news about William Jameson and Jerry Truman. He said, "Both of them told their stories and they matched up totally. As it turned out, Sgt. Carson had developed another plan for Father Bishop without telling William and Jerry what he was setting up. They did not know anything about your involvement with Sgt. Carson or the shooter.

"The District Attorney, Jennifer, told Jameson and Truman that they would not be charged for murder, since it appeared that they knew nothing about Sgt. Carson's plan to murder Father Bishop. She said that she would give both men consideration for their cooperation. They would instead be charged with stealing money from the church and the city.

"That left the matter of Sgt. Carson. I have looked for him, but his apartment looked like he had left with some of his belongings. I have put an all-points-bulletin out for him, but we have not gotten any feedback yet. That is where we stand now. It has been a good day for the good guys. Let's hope we can finish this off tomorrow or the next day. Keep a lookout for Sgt. Carson.

"We do not have any reason to think he knows where you live. But, Preston, be careful. I would not have considered him dangerous, but now I do not know what he may be capable of. I will talk to you sometime tomorrow. Have a good night".

Preston thought, that since he had the phone on speaker setting, Samantha probably heard everything. We looked at each other and she said that the end is in sight finally. I said, "I think I will get my gun out of my apartment just in case. I will be right back. It may be time for our first glass of wine for the night. I vote for a red wine".

I went to the apartment and got the 357-magnum pistol. I checked it to make sure it was loaded. For some reason the old saying that 'an unloaded pistol is an expensive paper weight' came to mind. I did not see anything else I needed so I stuffed the piston in my belt at my back from habit. On the walk back to the house, all the occurrences of the past few months came to mind. It was hard to imagine all that happened. Sometimes the mind really wanders. I thought of what you hear about friendships made in times of high stress often fade away after the stress subsides. That made me think of Samantha and my relationship. I fervently hope that maxim did not prove to be true in my relationship with Samantha. It had been so perfect. Thank goodness I finally got back to the house so these strange thoughts would stop. When I got back at Samantha's house, I pushed those scary thoughts out of my head.

When I opened the door and went in, I saw Samantha sitting in a chair in the corner. When I looked around the room, I saw Sgt. Carson standing there with his gun out. I blurted out the first thought that came to mind, "How did you find me Sgt. Carson? I know you found the GPS tracking device on your car, but how did you know I was here?"

He said, "You are a pretty good detective, but you are not the only one that knows some tricks. I remembered your tag number and did a search. You listed this address when you registered the vehicle. Sit down next to Ms. Carter. I want you to tell me where the investigation stands. What does Sean know?"

I said, "Sgt. Carson, I am not going to lie to you. The whole story is out. William Jameson and Jerry Truman have told the District Attorney everything. They will not be facing murder charges but will be held accountable for the theft of the church and city money. As far as you, Sean knows that you met with the shooter on two occasions. I am sure you know the shooter that you hired has been arrested. He was in possession of the rifle that killed Father Bishop and the pistol used to shoot Sean. The money he was paid for the shooting was also in his car. As you would expect, he is not admitting to anything, but I do not think that will matter. He will be found guilty. Sgt. Carson, I think that leaves you in a lot of trouble. Part of me had hoped you had managed to escape and leave the country, as difficult as that would be. So, what now?"

Sgt. Carson said, "None of what happened was planned from the beginning. The four of us were just trying to put aside some retirement money. It seemed like a good plan, but things changed. If I had been smart, I would have retired and taken my poor retirement fund and tried to get by. Looking back, I am sure the other two guys would say the same. But we find ourselves in a different situation. If I had not met you, everything would probably have worked out with no problems. I could be in South America on the beach now".

I spoke up, "Why are you here? Do you want to take revenge on me? If so, take me and let's go. Leave Samantha alone. She did not cause your problems. I will go with you willingly as long as you don't hurt her".

Samantha interrupted, "No, we are together. If you take him, you have to take me. If not, I will hunt you down or die trying. Just leave us and tell us how much head start you want. We will honor that".

Sgt. Carson turned to me and said, "Did you know that I was also in the Marines. I was in Vietnam for two years. I served my country, for 9 years. Now I have been a policeman here in Sandton for 35 years. I just wanted enough money to retire on. But that was not to be".

I waited several seconds and then replied, "Sgt. Carson, you did a bad thing, and it is irreversible. I respect your service in the Marines and your time in the police department, but that will not undo what you did. I have faced death many times as you did in Vietnam. We may have both done things that deserve death, but for some reason we were spared. The wrong thing you did here, cannot be undone, but you do not need to add more wrong things by harming Samantha and me. I ask you as a Marine to let us go and we will give you a head start. If you will not do that, then take me and do whatever you have to, but do not hurt Samantha. I suspect you have never hurt a truly innocent person. Let her go".

Sgt. Carson said, "I just cannot go to prison. I have sent too many felons there. I may be a coward, but I would rather die fighting one on one, not by a group of thugs. If I were to give you the gun, could you give me an honorable, quick death?"

I said, "No, Sgt. Carson. You are a fellow Marine, and I cannot do that. I understand what you are going through though. If you give me the gun, I will give it back to you with one bullet in it and you can leave. If you were to choose to turn yourself in and make a statement that will explain your dealings with the shooter, I would try to help you be sent to a prison out of state where no prisoners would know you or that you were a policeman.

Sgt. Carson held out his gun and said, "Take all the bullets out except one. I will leave and decide what I want to do. I am really sorry it has to end this way".

I answered, "Sgt. Carson, you have been a law enforcement officer most of your adult life. You can end it on a positive note by making sure that the shooter does not get away based on a lack of evidence". I took out all the bullets except one and handed it back to Sgt. Carson. He started for the door but stopped. He turned around and said, "Preston, I wish I had gotten to know you before all this mess started. You are very persuasive. You may have been able to set me straight. Semper Fi. Call Detective Murphy. See if he will agree to meet us here to take a statement. But he must come alone. If anyone else comes, there will be no statement".

I called Sean and told him the situation. He said he would be there in fifteen minutes, alone. He asked if everything was okay with us. I told him everything was stable and to make sure he was alone.

True to his word, Sean arrived in fifteen minutes. He came to the front door and knocked. We let him in and when he saw Sgt.

Carson he started to go for his gun. I spoke up and said, "Please Sean. Have a seat and take his statement. We have talked through this. He is not going to harm us. His gun has one bullet, and I think you know what that means. I have given him my word as one Marine to another Marine that if he gives his statement, he can take the gun with him or turn himself in, and I will help him go to a prison out of the state. If you cannot accept those terms, then you will have to leave without a statement".

Sean said, "I did not know that you were a Marine, Carson. I am sorry it has to end this way. I am here to take your statement, and I will abide by Preston's agreement with you. We have evidence against Bobby Sanford, but your statement will be a great help in closing this case. I agree with Preston that if you turn yourself in, we will try to help you, but I doubt there will be any deals that the district attorney will agree to other than possibility looking for an out of state prison".

Sgt. Carson said, "I understand and would not expect any deals. Let's get to the statement". Samantha got her laptop and Sgt. Carson dictated his statement. When he finished, she printed it out for him to read and sign if it was what he wanted to say. After he approved the statement, he handed it to Sean to review.

Sean said, "This looks like it will be sufficient. What do you want to do now?" Sgt. Carson looked at Sean, then looked at the gun in his hand and then handed it to Sean. He asked for a pen to sign the statement. The tension in the room noticeably diminished. Everyone took their turn telling Sgt. Carson that he had done the right thing. Samantha and I signed the statement as witnesses and dated it. Before Sean and Carson left, Carson asked for a pen and paper. He wrote out a bill of sale for his car. He said he had parked it one street over. He said he did not have any possessions except the car and that he would like Preston to have it, because he would have no use for it now. Sean said, "Sgt. Carson, I am going to violate police procedures and not handcuff you. I think you have earned that level of respect". They turned and left.

Samantha and I just looked at each other for a long time. Finally, Samantha spoke up, "Well, that was an unusual end of the day. That is going to be hard to top. I do have a $ 5 bottle of wine. We can celebrate the end of a great adventure".

I said, "Why do you have a $ 5 bottle of wine? You can afford better wine". She laughed and said, "It was intended for cooking, but will have to do because my hired help drank up all my good wine. The wine consumption around here has increased since you arrived. You should know that I was just using wine to reel you in. Now that I have you, you will have to start buying the wine".

I said, "What you are saying is that the price to get you is the wine. Is that one bottle of wine or more than one bottle? You realize that this is a negotiation process that we are in. I just need to know what I am getting into. Also, is the wine California or French wine? I think you are selling yourself short. I would have probably gone higher than a cheap bottle of wine". She said, "Drink your wine. I will show you what a bottle of cheap wind will get you".

CHAPTER 39

CASE CLOSED AND LIFE BEGINS

The next morning when we woke up, I said, "If last night was what a bottle of cheap wine gets me, I cannot wait to see what a $200 bottle of wine will get me". She grinned her typical grin and said, "It will get me for life".

We decided that we could go to the police station to see Sean since we were not confined to the house anymore. When we got to Sean's office, he said that he felt as though he was out of a job since the case was solved. He said, "Actually, I will have a lot of things to get ready for the trial, but I may have to think about a bigger city where there is more crime.

You and Samantha did such a good job that you will probably not have to appear in the court proceedings. With all the evidence and Sgt. Carson's statement, it should be an open and shut case. Bobby Sanford may plead guilty to try to get a little sympathy for a shorter sentence. I don't think that will help given what he did. If I were you, I would talk to the District Attorney to confirm that you will not be needed for the trial. I think I remember you have a honeymoon to complete".

I said, "You are correct. We will talk to Jennifer today. We do have a few things to take care of before we go on our honeymoon. We will keep you informed on our whereabouts. If there is nothing else you need from us, we will get out of your hair. Take care and do not work too hard".

As Samantha and I were walking down the hall to the police station exit, I said, "We need to plan where we want to go on our honeymoon. I promised you a honeymoon to remember so it will take some planning. There is one thing we have to do first though". Samantha looked puzzled.

I said, "What comes before a honeymoon? I do not want your buddy, Danny to come after me. We need to plan and schedule our wedding". Samantha agreed and said, "Since neither you nor I have any family, it may turn out to be a small wedding".

I said, "This is a first and last wedding for both of us. "We need to do it right. It does not have to be big, but you need a beautiful wedding dress, and I will need a tuxedo. I do have one problem. I need a best man. I only know two potential men, Sean and Danny. I guess Sgt. Carson would not be a potential best man. What would you suggest, Danny or Sean?"

Samantha said, that is up to you totally. I thought about it for a moment. I said, "Danny will probably walk you down the aisle, so I could have Sean as the best man".

Then I said, "Let's call Jennifer to confirm that we do not have to schedule around the trial. If the answer is no on the trial, I vote for a quick wedding so we can get started on the honeymoon". Samantha agreed, so I called Jennifer. She confirmed that she did not think we would be needed for the trial. She said she would let us know if things changed.

On the ride home, Samantha said, "Preston, I appreciate your concern about wanting to make this a beautiful wedding, but to be honest, that is not that important to me. I would settle for a justice of peace with maybe Danny and Sean there as witnesses. If it important to you to have the more formal wedding, I will go along, but do not do it for me. I consider us married now. We need to do the legal thing, but nothing about the ceremony will make me more committed to you and our marriage".

I said, "It would be okay with me if we see a minister on the street to get him to make it official. Seriously, I just suggested the formality for your sake. If you truly do not care for the big wedding, we can set up a preacher and have Danny and Sean attend as you suggested. That does mean that we need to do some quick scheduling of where we want to go for the honeymoon. That, we will not skimp on. As long as we are where they serve drinks with umbrella's I will be happy".

We set up the wedding ceremony for a week from today after making sure that the two witnesses could make it there. We got reservations for our honeymoon at St. Lucia.

There was one thing I decided that I wanted. I wanted to see and have pictures of Samantha is a beautiful white wedding dress. I told Samantha of my thoughts and she teared up and said that she would like that, but didn't want it to seem like she wanted a formal wedding.

That being settled we went to pick out her a wedding dress. The minute we walked into the wedding shop, Samantha's eyes fell on a dress that was elegant but not extravagant. It did not have a long train, but it looked like it was designed for Samantha. She asked what I thought.

I said that after you wear that, they need to destroy the pattern. You should be the only one to ever wear that design. It is beautiful and it is you. I realized now that I had to get a tuxedo. I did not want to look like hired help standing next to her. We finished our shopping and went back home.

We decided that with the wedding dress and my tuxedo, we would really need to have the wedding in our church. This then led to Samantha saying that we actually needed to invite some of her work friends. I certainly agreed that it would be nice and the appropriate thing to do. We then realized that we need flowers.

We began to think that we should have done more planning. We had been so happy about how the investigation turned out that we really just wanted to get married for appearance sake and begin out new life. No one else knew we were already married, even if it was only in our commitment to each other.

It was amazing that with all the planning we had not done, we were still able to pull it together in a couple of weeks. We managed to invite her friends and co-workers. Since I really did not have friends in South Carolina, it would be a small wedding, but neither of us cared about a big fancy wedding.

The day of the wedding came, and people kept coming into the church. Sean was to be my best man so I asked him who all these people were.

He laughed and said, "I mentioned that I need to take off today for the wedding to Chief Stone. He asked if I thought it would be alright for him and his wife to come. I told him that I thought you and Samantha would appreciate them coming. I hope I did not overstep my responsibilities as best man. I am not experienced in this responsibility.

I smiled and said, "It will be fine and a nice gesture."

Sean spoke up and said, "It may have gone a little further than that. That man and his wife coming in are Mayor Simpson and his wife. He said that this community owed you and Samantha a lot and he wanted to come. I am not sure who some of the others are, but I suspect they are people that Samantha has helped in her counseling. She is actually well respected in Sandton.

The wedding turned out to be more than what we had thought we wanted, but I was so glad that it worked out the way it did. Samantha was deserving a wedding like this and it all came together without the months of stress.

After the ceremony, we thought we would shake a lot of hands and say good by to everyone. What we did not know was that Sean, Chief Stone, Danny and the Mayor had other plans. They had arranged a reception and a local event facility, so we had a reception with everyone that attended the wedding.

At the reception, I was expected to make a speech to thank everyone. That went reasonable smooth. I turned to Samantha and asked if she would like to say anything. She stood up and fought back tears and expressed her appreciation for everyone sharing this time with us. After the applause, she wiped her tears and sat down. I likewise sat down.

The Mayor stood up and asked if he could say a few words. Samantha and I smiled and showed our agreement. He began,

"Preston and Samantha, many of us here were not officially invited to your wedding, but this community owes you both so much, we could not stay away. We felt we had to express to you how grateful we are to you for all you have done in the past few weeks. It is a small gesture, but we would like to give you the keys to the city and say that we are here to support you in any way we can. I am afraid we cannot name the city after you since it has been called Sandton for over 100 years. We are truly glad to have you as neighbors.

I felt I had to say something although that would be hard to follow. I stood up and said, "I am and I feel that Samantha is, as well, overwhelmed. Your generosity and kind words will be with us forever. When I think about how I chose to come to Sandton and to meet the one person that completed my life, I realize that Samantha and I are exactly where we are supposed to be. Thank you all.

The next week we met with Danny and Sean and told them how much they meant to us. After a few tears and well wishes, we then left to start out new life.

CPSIA information can be obtained
at www.ICGtesting.com
Printed in the USA
LVHW111053060123
736443LV00012B/511/J

9 781665 574709